LIN FINITY
IN
HOLDING ON

LIN FINITY
IN
HOLDING ON

A Fringes Of Infinity
Novella

Edward Allen Karr

LAKESIDE LETTERS, LLC

Lakeside Letters, LLC
30628 Detroit Road, #247
Westlake, OH 44145

This is a work of fiction. Names, characters, businesses, events, and incidents are the products of the author's imagination. Any resemblance to actual persons, living or dead, or actual events is purely coincidental. Certain long-standing institutions are mentioned, but the characters are imaginary. The opinions expressed are those of the characters and should not be confused with those of the author.

Lin Finity In Holding On
A Fringes Of Infinity Novella
©2020 Edward Sechkar.   All rights reserved.

First Edition, 2020
www.lakesideletters.com

Cover design by JD Smith Design
Front Cover Model: Kim Hendrickson as Lin Finity

ISBN-13: 978-1-950886-12-8

Other Books By Edward Allen Karr

* * * * *

SERIES: Fringes Of Infinity

Lin Finity And Her Mayhem Rising – Book One

Lin Finity And The Words Unspoken – Book Two

Lin Finity And The Islands Of Time – Book Three

Lin Finity And The Flights To Forever – Book Four

* * * * *

SERIES: Thrills N Kills In The Hills

Dayzee Dazzle And The Kildare Killers – Book One

Dayzee Dazzle And Her Manic Mansion – Book Two

* * * * *

DEDICATION

This work is dedicated to:

All who battle bravely
through every manner of adversity
and still . . .
never find their mayhem.

A deep and unending love,
deeper than the deepest ocean,
waits also for you.

"Does the freed balloon look only in the direction it floats when it becomes weightless? Or can it look back at the string that once held it securely and always remember a time before it began to drift? If it did that, could it carry a strong memory of being anchored to sustain it wherever it might travel? Could it hold that string itself, Lin?"

From Chapter 1 – Floating Off

x

Table of Contents

DEDICATION vii

Chapter 1 – Floating Off 1

Chapter 2 – Shoveling Snow 5

Chapter 3 – Giggling Again 13

Chapter 4 – Breaking Hearts 20

Chapter 5 – Taking Lives 28

Chapter 6 – Burying Mayhem 37

Chapter 7 – Falling Apart 47

Chapter 8 – Lingering Smiles 54

Chapter 9 – Meeting Nomad...61

Chapter 10 – Dressing Up 68

Chapter 11 – Driving Fast 73

Chapter 12 – Holding On...82

Chapter 1 – Floating Off

The moon poured its soft light over the gleaming hood of Lin's car, and her green eyes caught as much as the windshield would allow to bounce inside. In the rush to stop her hours-long flight into a sunset that had long ago yielded to night, she'd raced into a roadside rest area. But she hadn't bothered to park properly. Instead, she'd looped around to face east, and her Temt8tion remained alongside the rest area's curb nearest the highway, its two headlight beams burning parallel paths across the white lines of vacant parking spaces.

To her left, across the asphalt, a dense pine forest leaned heavily against the lot, grudgingly leaving a small space for a single picnic table. And along the tree line, far past the reach of the twin rays, a lonely moon rose above the treetops. To her right, beyond an expanse of wet grass, lay the still and empty highway—her escape route from the life she'd left behind.

Lin caught the last trace of a tear on a manicured fingertip before she grasped the steering wheel with both hands. She wondered if the moonlight had helped in chasing her tears back inside until they'd be needed once more. And she couldn't doubt that she'd have need of them again.

She shifted her legs and remained careful to not snag her black stockings under the steering column. The car's powerful engine idled a deep rumble, ready to resume her flight westward. Only a press on the pedal would be needed to continue their journey.

"It's a lot, I know, Lin."

She turned to her right and held the steady, calm gaze of Gabriel, the friend she'd known as Gabby since she was fifteen. She could only shake her head slowly as the memories of the last thirty-plus years, the sheer weight of them all, continued to reverberate through her. They flowed like a never-ending mountain stream fighting to squeeze through a passage only just wide enough to contain it. Still, a smile lit her face, and her eyes shined with a confidence and clarity that had been elusive since the day Gabriel had arrived.

"Yes, it really is a lot, Gabby. I don't understand how you just made me remember you and every part you've played in my life. You've always been a friend—my best friend—but I could never question anything about you. How I always saw you as real, but I never noticed that no one else even knew about you. How I didn't remember that horrible moment that brought you to me. How you've protected me and encouraged me to choose good, and all the while, I knew you only as some pleasant companion."

She looked back out over the steering wheel as her eyes filled with fresh tears.

"I think I know what you are, but I can't believe that you've spent over three decades watching out for me. All that time, Gabby!"

"It really has been a wonderful time for me, Lin. Please don't ever doubt that. The rest—your understanding and acceptance of it all—will come to you with time."

"I hope so. Right now, I feel that amazing power inside me—my mayhem—and I know I'll never lose it. It's unbelievable. But I also feel like a balloon whose string broke, and I'm floating off somewhere. I spent over thirty years not completely knowing what was going on in my life."

"Ah, Lin . . . do you think you ever will know completely?"

She wiped under her eyes and turned to face Gabriel again. She let out a short laugh and shook her head a few times.

"No, probably not. Not with what I've seen of the magic and what I can do with it. But most people go through life feeling like they know what's happening in their lives, don't they?"

"They think they know, Lin."

She stopped smiling and looked into Gabriel's big brown eyes.

"It's never that easy, is it?"

"No."

She looked out at a moon that she thought might be looking back at her, maybe even trying to understand her life, too, and she reached for the gear shifter with her right hand. But she only rested her hand on it. The engine continued its muffled thunder.

"Does the freed balloon look only in the direction it floats when it becomes weightless? Or can it look back at the string that once held it securely and always remember a time before it began to drift? If it did that, could it carry a strong memory of being anchored to sustain it wherever it might travel? Could it hold that string itself, Lin?"

"Maybe, Gabby, but it doesn't seem possible."

She allowed her hand to drop off the shifter and down to the center console. She felt it vibrating from an engine that waited patiently to be turned loose. She adjusted her blue beret and felt the comfort of the car's leather seat.

"Your memories of me have been restored. Really, though, they were never anywhere else but inside you. You needed to look away from them for a time, and that time came to an end only moments ago. It was time for you to remember who I really am. And now, you feel apart from your own life?"

"Boy, do I—I just left my entire life behind. But that's not it. I feel apart from *myself*, not just my life. Will that feeling pass?"

"Yes, I'm sure it will, Lin. This view of yourself, the way you see yourself only now, is entirely new to you. In time, you will feel a comfort again."

She sighed and looked to her right, past Gabriel, at the moonlit ribbons of concrete, and then up through the moon roof at a black dome dotted with only a few points of starlight. She bit her lip as she stared into the night.

"Sitting here in the darkness probably doesn't help, Lin. Who knew Pennsylvania could get so dark?"

"Oh, it sure can, Gabby. Cold too. It was so good to spend some time back in St. Simons Island last week. I'm glad I had that reunion as an excuse to go."

She turned to look out over her steering wheel.

"That's where I met you, but you weren't born there, were you?"

"'Met me?' Is that what you'd call it?" Lin said with a soft laugh.

"It was much more than that, but yes . . . that was our first meeting."

"Yeah, I guess you're right about that. No, I was born here, in Pennsylvania. We moved to St. Simons when I was ten. I remember at the time hating the idea of going. I had to leave all my friends, start a new school . . . all of that. I told my parents I wanted to stay, and I listened to their reasons for leaving. They were good reasons, and at that age, I couldn't think of any arguments other than that I didn't want to leave."

"Did you feel their love for you, Lin? Even though they were doing something you didn't want?"

"Yeah, of course. Looking back on it now, I see that their love was like a warm blanket, wrapped around me tight. The thing is, it was always there . . . every day of my life. That made it easy to lose sight of it. Does that make sense?"

"Sure, it's easy to take for granted. We're made that way."

"Not you, Gabby."

"I was like that too. Not anymore, though. Do you remember the day they told you that you were moving?"

"I haven't thought about it in ages, but yeah, I do remember. I realize now that they waited for the right time to tell me. I didn't know it then, though."

"What do you remember?"

Lin dropped both hands onto her lap.

"It was New Year's Day, the day after a blizzard like I'd never seen before. Snow had drifted so high I couldn't see over it. And even though the sun shined brightly, a cutting wind swept across the driveway, and I stood there holding a shovel in hands already going numb inside my mittens . . ."

Chapter 2 – Shoveling Snow

"That was good, Mom. I know some kids make fun of grilled cheese sandwiches, but I don't. I think they're good."

"I'm glad you like it, Hon. How about that tomato soup? Pretty good too, huh?"

"I liked it! Hot soup on a day like this—it's the best. Look at it out there, Mom. How could so much snow fall in one night?"

"Oh, Honey, that's Pennsylvania for you. You just never know. At least the sun is out, though. That's a good thing, don't you think?"

"It's kind of bright."

"Yeah, maybe you'll need your sunglasses, huh?"

"For what? I'm not going out there. It's too cold!"

Audrey Finnerty laughed and said, "You're right about it being cold out there, Honey. It's nice to know the whole entire world isn't this cold and snowy. There really are places that are warm, even right now. But not here. I think your dad was looking for you. Why don't you go see what he wants?"

"Sure, Mom."

Ten-year-old Lin took the basement stairs two at a time, and though she held her hand close to the rail, she never touched it. Even in winter, her father's rec room was always toasty and offered a permanent conglomeration of scents, reminding her of every good meal they'd enjoyed down there. The small television facing the two recliners showed one of his customary nature and travel shows.

Lin swept both legs up as she jumped and landed just right in her chair.

"Hi, Dad. Whatcha watching?"

Roger Finnerty grabbed up the remote and turned down the volume.

"Hi, my Lin. Oh, it's just some show about crows. I, for one, didn't know just how intelligent they are. Scientists have spent a lot of time studying them, and they can't figure out their language—not even close. They make too many distinct sounds. And you know what? If you take the time, they get to know you and trust you. Especially if you feed them."

"Pretty neat. How's your back?"

"Eh. It's not quite right yet. I should have been more careful on the stairs coming down here that day. I wasn't paying attention, and bam. Just like that. I hope you're always careful, Baby."

"Yeah, Dad, I am. Mom said you wanted to see me?"

"You've looked outside, right?"

"Yeah, Dad. There's a lot of snow!"

"And you know I can't shovel any of that, not today anyway. Think you can be a sport and give it a try?"

"Dad! There's too much!"

"Yeah, I know, I know. Hey, you remember in the summer, how we cleaned that driveway up real good?"

"Sure, with the hose, you mean?"

"Yeah, that was fun, wasn't it? Squirting the water in all the saw cuts and getting the dirt out of there?"

"Dad, I can't wash away all that snow!"

Her dad laughed and said, "No, Lin, it's about the cracks. Those cuts in the driveway."

"What about them?" Lin said as she kicked her legs up and down.

"Well, you remember how they make big squares out of the driveway?"

"Yeah, sure."

"What if you went out there, bundled up real warm, and you planned to clear snow off of just one of those squares? That wouldn't be so bad, would it?"

"It's still a lot of snow, Dad, but I guess shoveling just one square wouldn't be so bad."

"That's all I'm asking, Lin. One square. See how it goes, okay? I wish I could help . . . but not today, I'm afraid."

Lin glanced at her father's work boots, the ones he put on as soon as he got out of bed and didn't take off until the day was done. She knew he was a hard worker and would happily attack all that snow. But he couldn't.

"Okay, Dad. Just one square," she said and giggled as he shook his head and smiled.

"You're a special girl, my Lin."

Lin could only smile, and she swung her legs over the chair's arm and rolled up onto her feet.

"I wish I could do that," he said with a grin.

"You will, Dad. Right now, you're learning about crows."

After bounding up the stairs two at a time, Lin headed for the laundry room, where her coats and boots and hats and mittens were waiting. Her mom peeked in and watched her dress for a few seconds before she spoke.

"Hon, that's really good of you to try with that driveway. That's a lot of snow, though, so don't feel bad if you can't get much of it."

"Who knows, Mom? I'm sure dressed warm enough!"

"When you come back in, think you'll want some hot chocolate?"

"Oh yeah, Mom. Yeah!"

* * *

Lin hit the button to raise the heavy, frozen garage door, and she walked past her dad's old muscle car covered in a ratty green tarp. She ran her mitten over the entire length and imagined it polished up and racing in the sunshine, then she stepped into the wind and caught her breath.

Oh, this is too cold! she thought, and she retreated back out of the chill wind.

But only long enough to grab a shovel. For the first time, she looked at the drift from ground level and got a sinking feeling—she couldn't see over it.

Close to the garage, the snow barely covered the concrete, and she scraped enough aside to see the cut running down the middle from the house to the street. She took a second to look on each side of the line, to try to guess which side had less snow. She saw that it didn't matter—both sides had mountains of it, so she picked the left side, because she knew it could be seen from the living room window, and got started.

Where was that lousy line? she wondered as she picked away at the snow one shovel load at a time. Her arms felt it first, then her back. But she noticed something: she didn't feel the cold as much. So, she kept at it, and with a lot of effort, she'd reached her goal. She hid back out of the wind in the garage and looked at what she'd accomplished. One whole square was now snow-free, just like her dad had asked. She did that. All by herself.

She thought about the warmth of the house and her favorite mug full of hot chocolate. With marshmallows too! She turned to look at the door into the house, and a thought crept up on her: could she do one more square? Just one more, that's all. How bad could it be? Her dad would sure be surprised!

She'd already cooled down from standing still, so she snugged up the hood over her thick, wool hat, pulled the scarf back up to protect her face, and stomped back out to the next mountain of snow.

It wasn't easy since her body already ached, but she finished one more square and walked slowly back into the garage. She could almost taste the hot chocolate and feel the soft warmth of the couch.

How many squares were in that driveway? She thought back to cleaning it with her dad, riding her bike over it, and coloring it up with chalk, and she still didn't know. So, she looked at how big the square was and looked down to the sidewalk. There were twelve squares, she figured. Maybe she could do one more at least.

She kept at it until only two snowy squares remained. Lin heard her mom pounding on the living room window and turned to see her waving her in. But Lin shook her head and pointed at the snow. Her mom gave up and shook her head with a smile. Lin waved, took a deep breath, and returned to what she'd set her mind to do.

*   *   *

As soon as she walked in from the garage, both her mom and dad were there, though her dad was a little hunched over. But they both had huge smiles.

"Wow, my Lin, you're really something. How did you finish all that?"

"It wasn't easy, Dad, but I did it."

"Are you ready for that hot chocolate, Honey?"

"Yeah, Mom. I thought about that the whole time!"

"Aren't you tired after all that? I thought we figured you'd try one square and see how that went."

"I did, Dad. I tried one square, and then I thought . . . well, what if I try just one more? Just one more square?"

"And you kept going. I wouldn't have believed you could do that much. I never would have asked you to, that's for sure."

"At first, I didn't think I could either!"

*   *   *

Seated around the kitchen table, Lin looked out at the deep snow over the backyard, and she felt the pins and needles in her feet as the cold got chased out of them. When her mom set her Miami Beach mug with a smiling blue dolphin in front of her, and a bag of mini marshmallows, too, she smiled and forgot all about her aching muscles.

"Take a sip, Honey. It'll warm you up. Did you like being out there in the cold?"

"Not really, Mom, but I'm kind of glad I did all that. Snow isn't as much fun as it used to be."

"Yeah, it really isn't. That reminds me . . . there's something we want to talk to you about."

Lin stirred a few marshmallows into the steaming chocolate and blew on it.

"What's that, Mom?"

* * *

"That's when they told you about moving, Lin?"

"Yeah, Gabby. Right after I fought my way through a crazy amount of snow. Pretty smart, huh?"

"I'd say so, but you still weren't happy about moving?"

"Nope. But if I hadn't done all that work out there, I would have really hated the idea."

"They handled that well. And you said they really did need to move?"

"Yeah, for work. My dad didn't know for sure his back was ever going to get back to normal, and he wouldn't be able to work like he'd been doing. They thought there were better jobs for him down in St. Simons."

Lin felt the car rumbling beneath her as she stared out at the moon, which had climbed a bit farther into the night sky. She held the wheel with both hands and felt that the life she'd just left behind in Allentown was as far away as her childhood. The motor waited, and she slid her black heel across the carpet until she felt the toe pressed against the side of the gas pedal.

"They wanted your approval, though?"

"Yeah. Isn't that something, Gabby? I was just a ten-year-old kid— they didn't have to explain anything to me."

"That's love, Lin. Even though you weren't happy about it, did you agree to go?"

"I did. I saw how important it was to them, and I knew I couldn't really argue anyway. I was just a kid."

"Is it possible you were more than just a kid, Lin?"

10

She shook her head and continued gazing into the dark.

"I don't know, Gabby. Especially a couple of years after that. I felt more like a trapped animal than anything else. I wished to God I could be 'just a kid' again."

"When you shoveled more snow than you thought you possibly could, did that tell you something about yourself?"

"Oh yeah, it sure did. I didn't really think about it at the time, but I learned that if I apply myself to something, if I really focus on it, I can do way more than I think. I did get pretty sore, though."

She turned and smiled at Gabriel, who continued to look straight out into the night.

"You pushed yourself through something difficult, and you became stronger for it?"

"Yeah, that's for sure. I know what you're getting at, Gabby. It was the same way when I was twelve, but it was so, so much more difficult."

"And it led to something more than just sore muscles, didn't it?"

Lin looked back out through the windshield to see a bright moon raining its cold light all around them.

"Yeah. Boy, did it ever. It was a high price, though. I didn't think I'd make it, and you know, I wouldn't have without you."

"You would have been fine, Lin. It might not have been as much fun, though. I've been pretty good company, haven't I?"

She turned back toward Gabriel with a big smile. Gabriel turned and looked into her moistening eyes.

"As bad as it was, I wouldn't trade any of it, Gabby. I never would have found my mayhem, and I never would have met you. I can never tell you how much I appreciate all you've done for me."

"I've enjoyed it at least as much as you. Before things got bad, do you remember life in St. Simons? Did you enjoy the sunshine and warmer weather?"

"Oh, I sure did, and I never missed the snow. I can remember the first time I walked into the ocean. The sun was high in a clear blue sky, and my mom packed a lunch. I sat on the green blanket my mom laid

out, unlacing my shoes, and I felt hypnotized by the sparkling blue
waves . . ."

Chapter 3 – Giggling Again

"You look like you forgot how to blink, Honey," said Lin's mom.

Lin didn't answer. She fumbled with her shoelaces while staring at the ocean with her eyes stretched wide.

"I think she likes the ocean," said her dad with a smile while he worked at removing his boots.

"Lin, Honey, are you still with us?"

Lin shook her head a couple of times and looked over at her mom.

"Yeah, Mom. It's just . . . I can't believe how big it is. How could there be so much water?"

"Oh, my Lin," said her dad, "that's just a very tiny part of it all. How far away would you say Africa is from here?"

Lin turned back and looked farther out, and her open mouth appeared to be trying to form words, but all of her effort went to her squinting eyes.

"You can't see it, that's for sure. You should have watched that show with me the other night. I think they said it's about four-thousand miles from here. Think you can swim that far?"

Lin finally broke her stare, turned to her dad, and giggled.

"No, Dad, no one could! How deep is it? How far out can we walk?"

"It's pretty shallow here close to land, and it drops off pretty gradual, but you still can't walk out too far. Don't forget, Baby, there are sharks and all kinds of things in there."

"What kinds of things? Besides sharks?"

"Probably anything you can imagine is in there."

"Oh, Roger, what are you telling that girl? Hon, there are all kinds of happy fish and dolphins and things like that. As long as you stay close to the shore, you'll be fine. Why don't we walk out there a little ways?"

"Yeah, Mom! Let's go!"

Lin jumped up and dug her toes into the sand that was already hot from an ambitious March sun. She kicked at it while she waited for her parents to get up, and while holding their hands, they all hiked until their feet sank into the wet sand and waves rolled up and around their ankles.

"It's cold!"

"It's just too early in the season, Honey. It'll warm up. Maybe just walking in it is enough for today?"

"Okay, Mom. I think I'd freeze to death in there!"

They walked out far enough for the waves to wash up over Lin's knees, and she tugged her hands free. Her parents took a few steps back, and Lin could see nothing but water. With her arms raised to each side, she gazed out toward the horizon, and an Africa that she couldn't see, and felt her toes sinking in. She wiggled them to get them in deeper.

All that water, she thought, just sitting there, going all the way to Africa. Dad's right—there must be all kinds of things living in there. How would we even know what's down there? It's too deep! Anything could be hiding in there!

*　*　*

Back at the blanket, Audrey dug into the basket and found egg salad sandwiches for all of them. She kept looking and found potato chips and milk for Lin. She handed Roger a can of cola and uncapped her own bottle of juice. But Lin knew what it really was—it was wine. Lin was glad her mom was having her favorite drink while they all enjoyed the beach.

"I just can't stop looking at that," Lin said as she ate and stared at the sea.

"As long as you remember to eat, my Lin. You won't be shoveling snow anymore, but you do want to grow up strong, don't you?"

14

"Yeah, Dad, and I sure don't miss the snow, but tell me more about the ocean. Do we know everything that lives there? Are there other things in there we don't know about?"

"I think people have figured out most of what lives there, Lin, but in a place that big and that deep, can we ever know for sure? I see a big, deep mystery out there. So, who knows? Maybe you'll help figure it out someday."

"Me? How would I do that?"

"You can do anything you put your mind to, my Lin. But I do have a very important question for you."

"Oh no . . . what, Dad?"

"When you're done with that sandwich, how does ice cream sound?"

"Good! It sounds good! I want chocolate! Let's go!"

"Roger, maybe we—"

"We'll be fine, Audrey. Things will pick up. Watch and see."

"I'm getting chocolate—that's the best!"

"After your sandwich, Honey," said her mom.

*　*　*

The short hike to the Village took them under and around sprawling live oaks, and Lin ran her hand over each one and jumped up to touch the leaves. When they'd reached the ice cream shop's counter, she insisted on ordering her own.

"Chocolate for me! Two scoops!"

"Coming right up," said the young girl wearing a white shirt and curly red ribbons in her hair.

"And sprinkles!"

"Of course," said the girl with a smile. "You got to have sprinkles, right?"

Lin nodded, accepted the cone, and started on it right away. Her dad got a single scoop of vanilla, and her mom declined, saying she was fine with her juice.

"Can we walk to the pier, Dad?"

"Yeah, of course. Can't skip that, can we?"

"Nope." Lin smiled and shook her head and went back to her ice cream.

They'd moved into their new home on Palmetto Street just one week earlier, and that was the first chance they'd had to spend time in the Village and near the ocean.

There was school to get squared away, boxes to unpack, utilities to get going, and so many other things that Lin mostly tried to keep out of the way. But today was the first Saturday at the beginning of spring break, and they had time for the outing that Lin had been anticipating since they'd first told her that they were moving near the ocean.

Her mom had shown her photos of the pier, so Lin knew what to expect, but she couldn't help running ahead to get to it first. She'd forgotten about the cone in her hand, but the sensible reflexes of a girl that liked chocolate ice cream would never let it tip.

As she approached the rail farthest from land, Lin remembered her ice cream, and a few quick bites later, it was only a sweet, chocolatey memory. She stared out at the ocean again, from higher above the water than at the beach, and she still couldn't see Africa. But she could see endless blue in two shades: the water and the sky. She watched the thin line that separated them as it bounced so softly she thought that her eyes were playing tricks on her. But those were waves, she knew—waves so far away that she couldn't even imagine it.

She looked down at the water splashing up against the concrete below her, and she knew it wasn't very deep there. But she still couldn't tell what might be in there. Could something be looking back up at her, even now? Was something in there watching her? How would she ever know?

She looked farther out. Not as far as the horizon . . . just a place that she believed might be deep. She thought of being there, floating on that wave, and knowing that so much water dropped down to some dark bottom. And in between, from the surface to the very bottom, how many things were swimming past her? What were they all doing down there?

Looking down again from the rail, she imagined herself in the water, below the surface, and looking up. If she lived in there, she wondered, would she sometimes gaze up into the sky and wish that she knew what types of creatures lived there? If she lived in the ocean, what type of creature would she—

"Lin, you really do love the ocean! You might miss Pennsylvania sometimes, but this is pretty nice, isn't it?"

"Yeah, Dad. It's amazing. And look at the water—it's so calm."

"Not always, though, right? I know you know about hurricanes. We watched that show the other day. You remember?"

"I remember. I can't even imagine a storm that big. And that comes from the ocean?"

"Not just the ocean. It's a bunch of things: the heat, the wind currents, sunshine . . . all of it teams up sometimes and BOOM!"

"BOOM is right! I like it better like this. A storm that big is scary. But a storm like that starts there, out in the ocean?"

Lin pointed out over the water.

"Yeah, Lin, but not today. Today's a good day for ice cream. Was yours good?"

Lin giggled again and said, "Chocolate is always good, Dad. You know that!"

"Yeah, I do know that. I bet you'd like to come back here again sometime, huh?"

"I don't think I'll ever get tired of it, Dad."

* * *

Roger pried his daughter away from the rail, and since Audrey had finished her juice, she was ready to go too. They took a drive up Kings Way, then north on Frederica Road. A few miles later, he turned left on Palmetto, and seconds later, he pulled in their driveway.

"I like our new house, Dad. I think it'll feel like home real quick."

They walked up onto the porch, with Lin taking two steps at a time, and her dad unlocked the door. She walked in first and liked the squeaking sounds her sneakers made over the clean wood floor. Her mom brought the basket into the kitchen, and Lin looked in to see her pouring another glass of juice.

"Dad, what's on TV tonight? Any shows about hurricanes?"

"I don't know, kiddo. I'll check the listing and see what's on."

"You should take your shower now, Honey. You probably have some sand on you from the beach."

"I think I do, Mom. It's kind of itchy now that I notice it."

"Hey, Lin, there's a show on later about sea turtles. You want to watch that with me?"

"Yeah! I love sea turtles! Do I have time to take a shower before it starts?"

"It won't be on for an hour yet. Take your time. I'm glad we can watch that together, Baby."

*   *   *

"It sounds like you were having a pretty good life there, Lin."

"It was, Gabby. For a while anyway. You know, I've never gotten over how I felt looking out at all that water. When I was back there last week, I spent time standing in the exact same spot as when I was ten."

"You weren't quite the same person, though."

"No, and I still hadn't figured out my mayhem. I looked at the ocean, and I still had those same feelings about the mysteries that might be hiding out there. And this time, when I knew there was something going on with me, I felt like I was the same way too—that I had mysteries just like the ocean. Big mysteries."

"How do you feel now?"

"Like I figured out some of it, but I think there might be so much more. That's never going to change, is it?"

"No. We have to get used to that."

"And back then, when I was a kid staring at the sea and wondering about its mysteries, I had no idea what was ahead of me."

"How could you?"

"And you know what? Thinking about it here and now, I feel sad for that ten-year-old girl. She had no clue what kind of hell was coming for her."

"No, she couldn't know. If you could speak to her now, what would you tell her?"

Lin saw the two headlight beams tunneling into the night soften, and their edges became blurry. The first tear spilled out and trickled down her cheek, and she let it go where it wanted.

She looked up at the moon, now higher in the sky, and she sensed no understanding from it. Certainly no compassion. It was beautiful. And indifferent.

"I wouldn't tell her to run, and I wouldn't tell her to hide."

Gabriel waited quietly.

"I'd tell her that she needs to stay strong, because that's what carries us through our lives. I'd tell her that there's a strength inside her like she's never known possible—a strength and power so big that no one will ever, *ever* be able to hurt her again."

Gabriel nodded and turned to look at Lin.

"I'd tell her that there's love waiting for her on the other side of it. A love that she can't imagine right now. A love so deep and unending that she can't even conceive of it. Deeper than the deepest ocean."

She turned to face Gabriel, and thin trails of tears on each cheek reflected the strengthening moonlight.

"Anything else, Lin?"

"Yeah. I don't feel only sad, Gabby. I feel mad as hell."

Gabriel nodded and held her gaze.

"And what else would you tell her?"

Lin turned to look back out through wet eyes over the steering wheel at the cold pavement. She gripped the wheel tightly and spoke in a voice calm and forceful but not much higher than a whisper.

"Keep cutting."

Chapter 4 – Breaking Hearts

"How was school today, my Lin?"

"It was okay, Dad. Did you put that piece of chocolate in with my lunch?"

"I sure did. As long as I'm packing those for you, you can expect a special treat every once in a while."

"Thanks, Dad. That was a nice surprise. You pack lunches almost as good as Mom used to."

"Thanks. I think. Are you getting enough to eat?"

"Yeah, my lunches are fine. Sometimes after dinner, I'm still hungry."

"I know, Baby. We'll have more soon, I promise. You have about an hour before we eat. Do you have homework today?"

"A little. Maybe I'll go do that."

"Good. Learning is important."

Lin grabbed her school bag and bounded up the stairs two at a time. She felt her leg muscles working, and she couldn't race up the stairs as quickly with her backpack full of books, but she smiled by the time she reached the top.

Her bedroom sat at the rear of the house and faced south. Being only April, the sun still sent enough light through her window to warm a bright patch on the area rug that filled most of the room. After tossing her things onto the bed, she grabbed her brush, a small mirror, and the lipstick she'd taken from her mom's room the week before, and sat in the sunshine.

She'd just turned twelve, and though her mom didn't think she was ready for any kind of makeup, Lin knew she was. Her mom seemed too tired to ever notice that one missing item anyway.

She thought about the present she'd opened just the day before. She remembered trying to hide both laughter and tears when she opened the poorly wrapped package and found coloring books. She was twelve now! Practically a grown woman!

But she hid her shock and acted happy, and later, she thought through it and realized that her mom didn't buy the present. She was too tired. She was always sleeping, it seemed. And lately, her dad seemed more tired too. So, she tried to be happy with it. Coloring was still fun, she told herself. But sitting in the sunshine, in her quiet upstairs bedroom, she'd reached for the brush and lipstick instead.

First, she pulled her blond hair forward past her shoulders and checked the length. Good. It was growing. It was getting almost as long as she thought she'd want it, and she smiled into the mirror when she had to admit to herself that she kept adding to her goals for hair length. Someday, it'll be long enough, she told herself.

She gave all of it a good brushing and reached for the lipstick. Just for fun, she put it on heavy, smacked her lips together, and took a look. She liked it, and after a glance at the clock, she figured just how many minutes she could leave it like that before going downstairs for dinner. She knew that she'd leave it on as long as possible.

The backpack was close enough that she could stretch over, keeping her bare legs in the sunshine, and pull out a book that contained her reading assignment. Between peeks in the mirror, she finished the chapter and found that she actually liked it. It wasn't as fun as fiction, but the story of a veterinarian and all the animals she saved struck a chord. If only the animals all lived in the sea, she thought and tossed the book onto the bed.

"Lin," she heard her dad call up the steps. "Five minutes, okay? Dinner time."

"Okay, Dad."

She grabbed a tissue and began smudging off the lipstick, but not all of it. She'd been leaving a little bit more each time, and she always held her breath, hoping neither of them would notice it. They never did.

Well, maybe her dad did, she thought, but he never said anything. Maybe he liked her growing up. Her mom never paid that much attention. Not lately.

* * *

"This is good pizza, Dad. I never get tired of it."

"Well, you know, I'm not much of a cook, Lin, and I like pizza too."

"It's always a favorite of mine too," said her Uncle Ray.

Lin's father's brother Ray had moved in with them a month before. Her dad had explained the reason why, even before Ray had arrived. Her dad's back had gone bad again, and he'd lost his job. He didn't explain every detail to her, but she figured it out. There wasn't much money with her dad out of work and her mom too tired to work, and Ray seemed to have plenty. She guessed that he was helping pay the bills, which she knew made good sense.

But she didn't like him. He acted nice enough, but something in his eyes didn't seem right. Mostly when he looked at her, but not only then. He always seemed like he had a secret—something that he didn't want to tell anyone but something he was probably happy about. She'd learned right away that looking him in the eye was a bad idea. He looked back too long, and it gave her chills.

She looked over at her mom, who stared at her plate and ate slowly. Her glass of juice was almost empty, and Lin knew that she'd make an effort to refill it. That always seemed pretty important.

"Did you get your homework done, Sweetheart?"

"Yeah, Dad. I read about a veterinarian and all the animals she saved. It's pretty cool. I thought the only way it could be better was if she worked on things that lived in the ocean."

"There are doctors that do that, you know. Maybe you'll want to be a doctor like that when you grow up?"

"Maybe, Dad. It just seems so far away until I'm *that* grown up."

"You're wise beyond your years, Lin. Just enjoy your childhood for now. There's plenty of time to think about what you'll want to do with your life."

Lin nodded while taking another bite. And she felt like laughing—she was getting away with wearing lipstick!

"You'll be grown up before you know it, Lin," Ray said as he grabbed the last piece of the small pizza that they all shared.

Lin's smile inside vanished. Not because she was still hungry and wished she'd gotten to that slice first. Not because she thought Ray's money should start buying more food either.

"But right now, I'm only twelve. I'm not in a hurry to grow up."

She'd never looked at his eyes.

* * *

"Did you know dolphins weren't fish, Dad? I didn't know that."

"Yeah, I read that a long time ago. How about that, Lin? They breathe just like us, but they can hold their breath a long, long time."

"They said ten minutes. Some even up to fifteen minutes! That's amazing, Dad."

Lin stared at the commercial playing on the TV, eager for the show to continue. She felt her stomach grumbling, but she ignored it.

"That seems like a miracle to me, Sweetheart. The more I learn, the more this world surprises me."

"Does Mom know about dolphins and how long they can stay underwater? Maybe I should—"

"No, Baby, Mom's resting. And there's something I wanted to tell you. Tomorrow morning, I'm bringing Mom to the hospital for some tests. The doctors want her to stay a couple days. Not dolphin doctors, though."

Lin tried to giggle, but it didn't come out right.

"She hasn't been feeling well, and this is important to figure out what's going on. I plan to stay with her through the afternoon, so I won't be here when you get home from school. Don't worry, okay? Just come home like any other day?"

"Sure, Dad," she said and thought about going right upstairs and playing with her lipstick, especially since they wouldn't be around to walk in on her.

"You'll be fine—your Uncle Ray will be here to watch you in case you need anything."

Oh yeah, Lin remembered. Uncle Ray will be here. Fine, I'll just sneak upstairs real quick and maybe never even see him.

"Luanne's mom will drop you off like usual, won't she? Will that be alright?"

"Yeah, I always get a ride with Luanne. I'll be fine."

"This is pretty important, and I hope you're not worried about it."

"It's okay, Dad. Is Mom okay? Why is she tired all the time?"

"That's what we're going to find out. Don't worry, alright?"

"I won't. I'll be glad when she isn't so tired anymore."

"Me too, Baby. Me too."

*　*　*

Lin climbed into the backseat of Luanne's car, shuffled over to make room for Luanne, and said, "Hi, Mrs. Hicks."

"Hi, Lin. How was school today?"

"Good."

She'd dropped her backpack onto the floor and powered her window down. The afternoon heat had warmed the car, and Mrs. Hicks knew that Lin would rather have her window down than put on the air conditioning. Especially where Sea Island Road passed through the marshes with a gentle, sweeping turn to the right.

Within minutes, they'd reached Lin's favorite part of the drive, and she stared out at the water and plants and all the fish and things she could imagine living in there. She felt the car slow, like it always did, because Luanne's mom knew how special it was to her.

When they passed over the Mackay River, she climbed up onto her knees to get a better look at the water, hoping she'd see a dolphin pop up out of there and chatter at her, inviting her in for a swim. But she knew she'd never see a dolphin in there—it was only a nice childhood dream.

With the river behind them, Lin settled back into her seat. Seconds later, they turned left onto Frederica, then Palmetto, and the ride ended abruptly with the brakes squealing in front of Lin's house.

"Thanks, Mrs. Hicks. Bye, Luanne. See you tomorrow."

"Bye, Lin. I'll pick you up at the usual time tomorrow."

"Bye, Lin. I'll see you tomorrow, okay?"

"Okay."

Lin slammed the car door, swung her backpack up over her shoulder, and smoothed down her plaid skirt. There were only four steps to get onto the porch, and Lin jumped as high as she could and took three of them at once. Feeling satisfied that someday she'd somehow jump up all four of them, she hopped up the last one and walked across the porch. The door was unlocked, so she swung it in and aimed for the stairs.

"Lin, you're home."

Lin stopped.

"Yep, school's done."

She didn't want to do it, but she looked at his eyes. She regretted it—they were worse than normal. She felt the hairs on her neck straightening out, as if trying to escape and leave her on her own. He gazed at her without blinking, but Lin noticed what seemed like it might be a smile—one that he couldn't hide completely.

"Why don't you have a seat, and tell me about your day?"

Lin sat on the couch with her backpack on her lap, covering her bare knees, and minutes later, her childhood died.

* * *

"Lin, I'm sorry you had to live through that."

"Me too, Gabby. I'm not telling you or anyone else any details. But believe me, I remember it all—every rotten thing about that man, who I didn't like or trust from the beginning. When I look back at it now, I don't force myself to relive any of it, but I feel every bit of the pain, the fear, and the humiliation. I've come to accept it as if that man were punching me in the face over and over again. I can add real memories if I want to, but I don't need them. I add up all the feelings that I had starting that day, and together, they all add up to a grown man punching a twelve-year-old girl in the face. Each punch pushed me further and further, and after a couple of times, I thought that I could see a safe place—a place where I could hide and not feel the punches."

"But you wouldn't let yourself go there, would you?"

"No, Gabby. Sometimes, I felt stupid for not hiding. I mean, I just kept turning my face up to get punched again. I never let myself quit. I always felt I could take another punch if I had to."

"Like shoveling another square on your driveway?"

Lin turned, wiped at her eyes, and stared at Gabriel.

"Yes, that's it. I forgot that I made that connection even back then. Wow, Gabby."

"When you shoveled all that snow, more than you thought you could, did you feel stronger?"

"Yeah, I sure did, and it was the same with Ray. I knew I'd get stronger. I wanted nothing more than to be strong enough to stop him. I had a weird idea of being so strong that I'd make him stop himself. It didn't make sense to me, but I never quit believing that I was getting stronger. That's what I focused on."

"And you couldn't tell anyone?"

"No. At least, I didn't believe I could then. Maybe now, I'd know better and figure something out. Hell, now I'd destroy him in a heartbeat. Broken hearts or broken bones, Gabby."

Lin took a deep breath and let it out. The moon had risen higher, and she leaned toward the windshield to get a full view of it. It still didn't appear to have any interest, even though it must have witnessed all of the darkness that had flooded her young life.

"I knew Ray meant what he said. I didn't think about it this clearly, but even if I would have had him arrested somehow, my parents were still in trouble. As a family, we needed him to help with the bills. So, I took punch, after punch, after punch, after . . ."

Lin finally had to inhale, and she felt a fresh tear warming her cheek. She sensed Gabriel watching her in the moonlit car, and she knew how much Gabriel cared. Even though Gabriel might not show it, she felt there might be a heart breaking in her best friend beside her.

Chapter 5 – Taking Lives

"Happy birthday, Lin," Mrs. Hicks said after Lin had climbed in the backseat.

"Thanks, Mrs. Hicks."

Luanne said, "Lin, we're both fourteen now—we're practically grown up! It's about time, and next year, we'll be starting high school!"

"Yeah, you're right. I guess it's good to be grown up."

"Are you okay, Lin? What's wrong?"

"I just get tired sometimes, that's all. Mrs. Hicks? Can we drive slower through the marshes today?"

"Sure thing, Honey. We'll barely crawl down the road. How does that sound?"

"Thanks, Mrs. Hicks."

With the car inching along like a giant turtle, a fun image that Lin hadn't thought of in many months, she stared out over the calm high tide waters flooding between the thick plant life. The car startled a small squabble of gulls, and they flew away from the car, only inches above the marsh.

"I bet you wish you could live out there, huh, Lin?"

"Yeah, Luanne," Lin said without any real focus, "but there's more snow to shovel."

"Huh? What do you mean?"

Lin shook her head, but never looked away from the marsh.

"Nothing. Just thinking of a time when I was a kid."

* * *

"Well, you two girls, you made it through your freshman year. Congratulations!"

"Thanks, Mom."

"Thanks, Mrs. Hicks."

"We can take a special ride home if you'd like, Lin. How about if we ride up Ocean and take a peek out over the water? I know how much you like that."

"Oh, thanks, but that's okay. The usual route home is fine."

"Okay, Lin, but I'll slow down really slow through the marshes. We can at least do that, okay?"

"Sure. That would be nice."

Lin stared out through her window behind the driver's seat of Mrs. Hicks's car and barely heard Luanne continue a conversation with her mom. And when they rolled through the marshes, she hardly noticed the water and plants and birds.

But she did feel something moving inside her. She knew that it wasn't an upset stomach . . . nothing like that. It seemed that she'd become made of large pieces, not just one solid piece that was a girl named Lin.

She felt the places where the pieces joined together, like odd-shaped blocks that should be resting against each other, with no empty spaces between them. But they'd pulled apart and were moving around inside. She fought to not say anything, because how could she? What would she say? No one would understand. She didn't understand either.

A large piece, maybe the biggest one of all, twisted and turned, and Lin imagined it was pushing its way around, looking for a comfortable spot. Her insides were like the deep sea, where it was too dark to know what was there. This piece was the biggest and strongest, and maybe it was a shark. It knew where it wanted to be, and nothing could stop it— not the smaller fish, not the currents, not the tides . . . nothing. It was so big, so powerful, that no one could stop it. It felt like that, that piece inside her.

So, she let it go where it wanted, and she didn't tell Luanne or her mom. She wouldn't tell her parents when she got home, either, because they were off at their jobs.

She knew only that trying to stop it would be wrong because it had to find where it belonged.

When they'd passed over the Mackay and would soon turn onto Frederica, she knew there would be more punches waiting for her. And though she found no happiness or comfort in it, she knew that she could shovel snow forever.

If she still had to.

*　*　*

Lin stood on the sidewalk and listened to Luanne's car pulling away on Palmetto. She couldn't turn to look—too much was going on inside. The largest piece, the one that shifted and twisted to find where it belonged, seemed to have grabbed a few others to its cause. Together, they formed a much bigger thing, and Lin imagined that the giant shark had been devouring all the other fish around it. Soon, it might have them all.

She walked up to the base of the porch stairs and stopped to look down on them. She moved her feet closer together and felt the weight of her backpack slung over her shoulders. Slowly, she crouched down until she was almost sitting on the warm concrete, and she waited there, staring at the porch four steps up.

The shark seemed comfortable with all that it had taken inside itself. It still swam a little, but not much, and Lin felt that she might again be a single piece named Lin. Maybe a different Lin now.

Without a thought, and with her sights only on the porch, Lin's strong legs sprung her forward and up, and she landed where she wanted to be—on the porch. She'd somehow leapt over all the steps, even with her bulky books. No thought of self-congratulating even entered her mind. Instead, she looked to the doorknob.

The shark inside, the single piece named Lin, seemed to be waiting patiently, and it was more powerful than before. More powerful than anything. Lin turned the knob, pushed the door in, and stepped inside.

Her uncle Ray stood with a big smile at the far end of the small living room. Lin felt nothing as she closed the door behind her and dropped her bag. Thoughts of punching and shoveling had become the distant sounds of gulls on the horizon over her marshes, too far away to be heard.

But in fact, Lin had no wish to hear birds or anything else, and she saw only the eyes of her uncle leering at her from across the room. He took one step closer. His boot made a sickening click on the hardwood floor.

And Lin felt a tide rising inside her, coming from some unknown place deep within that large, now motionless piece she'd become. It swelled and grew and made her smile because the pressure of it chased away any fears or doubts that still lingered. She knew that sharks lived that way—without fear or doubt.

In an instant, she felt like she might burst, and she saw that Ray's eyes no longer leered. They still pointed only at hers, but the blood had drained from his face. His skin sagged, his mouth hung open, and he shook his head slowly.

The pressure grew to an uncontainable level as Lin stared at her uncle. Then, it felt like a gentle unmooring, a soft breaking loose, and she felt herself carried on an immense wave that exploded out from her in every direction.

She watched as his entire face froze into a soundless scream. Streaks of red took root in his bulging eyes, which shifted and twitched and appeared ready to slide out onto his cheeks. Lin felt no compassion—it was only proof of the power of the shark within her.

She rode that wave to him, and in some impossible way, she looked across the room to see herself standing there looking back. She saw that she was grinning, and her eyes burned with a fiery green light.

Lin accepted it without a single question. No fear. No doubts.

It was time.

She intended her uncle to walk into the kitchen, and his body responded. She heard him screaming quietly inside the life that she'd taken from him, but it didn't slow her down. He needed to scream, she knew. He could never scream enough for all that he'd done. And for all that he'd never do again.

His screams carried the desperation of a madman when she turned his eyes to the rack of knives on the counter. He might not have wanted to walk to them, but he had no choice. Lin had taken his life.

Standing calmly on the kitchen floor, screaming in a strange, silent way that Lin could somehow hear, he couldn't resist reaching out with his right hand to take the largest knife. She brought his hand up so that his eyes could get a good, long look at it. His left hand was getting things ready.

Feeling no doubts and using him like a puppet, with a surety as if she'd done it thousands of times, Lin forced him to begin lowering the knife. His silent screams became silent shrieks, and she felt the quiet sounds echoing inside her, touching her in strange ways. But it never slowed her down.

It could have taken only one quick slice, but Lin made Ray saw very slowly. Back and forth with the serrated blade, over and over. His silent shrieking had become the aimless cackling of an insane man.

When the last thread of flesh had been stretched tight and slit, she made him drop it with a splash on the floor. She felt him trying to look away, but he couldn't. Instead, she forced him to keep staring at what he'd butchered and watch his blood splatting into a syrupy puddle that sent one thick stream under the stove.

She left the dripping knife in his hand.

After she thought he'd seen enough, she intended damage to his eyes, and it felt like she was holding a graceful plant stalk from her marshes in each hand. Their structure felt delicate, a true gift of creation, and she clenched her fists and snapped them both. She knew that his eyes would never locate another victim. His creepy eyes could never again focus on her, and not on anyone else, or anything at all.

And his voice—that sneaky, scary voice . . . she aimed her intent at ending his voice so that no one would ever hear it again. She'd pulled weeds around their house when her dad needed help. It felt like that—like getting a nice grip on something that had no value, working it around a little bit, then ripping it loose. It felt good. The odd silent shrieking persisted, though.

She resisted the urge to destroy his mind. She knew that she could squeeze inside his head, just squish it all up like a handful of sloppy pudding. But she wanted him to remember all that he'd done and how he'd ended up. He might even continue to have his same twisted desires, too, and maybe that was okay. The evil would just bounce around in a hollowed out shell with no chance of becoming reality.

His capacity to feel pain . . . she left that. She left that working perfectly.

Lin paused after completing her work, and she took note of what she'd accomplished: he'd been mostly blinded, he'd never speak again, he'd remember what he'd done and the price he'd paid, and the pain would never stop. She gave him the final command to remain standing.

Lin had destroyed him.

* * *

Like a stretched rubber band snapping itself back, Lin got yanked into her own body. She looked toward the doorway to the kitchen, and a satisfied and relieved smile sprang up at the knowledge that her ordeal had ended. Ray would never hurt anyone again.

The smile vanished seconds later when she recalled the brutality of what she'd just done. And the unexplainable way she'd done it hit her like a hurricane.

How did that just happen?

How was that even possible?

Did I really do that to him?

What did I do?

What am I?

The questions attacked her from every direction as her heart raced and her breaths wheezed in and out. She tried to remain standing, but her strong legs went weak, and the room continued to spin about her even after she'd collapsed.

Before she lost consciousness completely, she felt the terror, the impossibility, and the insanity of what she'd just done. She lay there with her eyes unblinking, in a dead silent house, knowing exactly what horrors stood mutely bleeding in the next room.

Left with only one possible conclusion—that she was a monster—Lin closed her eyes and let her head rest on the wood floor, and she welcomed her slow spiral into a numbing darkness.

*　*　*

Lin awoke and felt wrapped in a fluffy beach towel under a warm sun. She listened for the sounds of waves or gulls, but there was only silence.

She opened her eyes to see that she was cradled in strong, gentle arms and surrounded by the softness of brilliant white feathers. She looked up and met the gaze of the kindest eyes she'd ever seen. She felt herself being rocked gently.

"It's okay, Lin. I'm here."

Her mouth quivered without making a sound, and she stared through eyes leaking out thick salty tears.

"I'm here for you, Lin. I will not leave you."

"Who . . . who are you?"

"I am Gabriel. Rest now."

She felt her heart calm, and she began to take slower, deeper breaths. She tried to speak again, or at least keep looking into the deep love that she saw in those timeless brown eyes, but she couldn't. Safe in a warmth and comfort not possible on any Earth she could imagine, Lin slept.

*　*　*

"And by the time my dad woke me up, you were gone, Gabby."

"Not really, Lin, but you know that."

"No, you're right—you were still there. You were with me. I'm glad you still let me call you Gabby, even now. I think I started that because it was all too much. It made it all seem less serious."

"I like the name. The name Gabriel is much more serious. My existence is mostly about very serious things."

"Except for me?"

"No, Lin. You and your life are very serious. And important. That's why I'm here. That's why I've been with you for over thirty years."

"I still can't believe I'm that important. I know that when I first met you, I couldn't have gone on by myself. I felt crazy even for a while after you showed up."

"Yes, I know."

The moon had traveled a bit to the right over the trees, and it was higher in the sky. Lin wondered if moonlight had any warmth to it, even if it was too weak to feel. Maybe its pale light only touches our hearts, she thought.

"Life went on after that. I felt you with me and helping me, but I still remembered all of the abuse, and I couldn't figure out how any of that had happened to Ray. None of what happened made sense. I still felt kind of crazy, Gabby."

"You never told anyone about any of it?"

"No. Right after I destroyed Ray, I knew I couldn't tell anyone about it. It didn't make any sense, and it was over—why upset my parents too?"

"You're very strong, Lin. Then, you had a confrontation with a classmate."

"Oh yeah, I sure did. It wasn't long after what I'd done to Ray."

"Do you remember that day now?"

"Yes. I knew about it all this time, but not the details of what I did to him. Not until you did whatever it is you just did—making me remember."

"That day started out fun, didn't it?"

"Oh, it really did. It was a Saturday at the beginning of summer break from school, and I was spending a lot of my free time with Luanne. She came by one day to pick me up with Ben and two other boys from school. The plan was to go to the Village and eat and see what was going on there. But I had a better idea. My mom and dad had taken off to pick up test results, so I grabbed two six-packs of my dad's beer. Maybe I shouldn't have taken that beer . . ."

Chapter 6 – Burying Mayhem

"Come on, Lin, let's go! It's already hot out! Ben's got his dad's car—he's right out front!"

Lin peeked out through her front door over Luanne's shoulder and saw the big sedan idling in the street. Two other boys waved from the backseat.

"Who's with him?"

"Just Floyd and Lucas. You remember them, right? From the operetta practice?"

"Oh yeah, those two guys. Okay, it'll be fun, but you know what would be more fun?"

"No, what?"

"Let's go up Lawrence to a place I know. It's Saturday, and probably no one will be around. It'll be even better than the Village."

"I don't know, Lin. What kind of—"

"Hang on. Wait right there."

Luanne turned to wave to the boys with one hand while she twirled around her curly blond hair with the other. Lin returned with two six-packs of beer and pushed her way out onto the porch. Before she could lock the door behind her, Luanne spoke up.

"What's that, Lin? You took that? Won't your dad know?"

"I don't think he cares anymore—not after all that's happened."

She handed Luanne one of the six-packs, pulled the door shut, and turned the knob to check that it was locked.

"That was just a week ago, Lin. Are you sure you're okay? Maybe you shouldn't be drinking?"

She grabbed the beer back from Luanne.

"I'll be fine. I just can't sit still in the Village. Let's go have some fun."

Lin jumped down over all of the steps and headed for the car, with each arm swinging a cold six-pack.

"You sure you're okay, Lin? After all that happened? That was just last week!"

"I'm going crazy just sitting around," she said over her shoulder. "Come on, let's just go."

* * *

"You did need to have some fun, Lin. I was happy to see you seeking some relief."

"I bet you weren't happy that I grabbed that beer, though, huh?"

"I wasn't surprised. You understand now just how much you went through and how impossible your life must have seemed. Drinking beer with friends doesn't have to be a bad thing."

"No, not until I made it bad. That wasn't the plan, Gabby. I remember how I felt back then. I don't think I had any control at all."

"Learning takes time. You had to begin somewhere."

"But not at someone's expense."

Lin looked out at a moon that she realized didn't care about her in any way. Not like Gabriel. No one could ever care about her like Gabriel did. She thought of how much damage her power could do and how she didn't have a mature understanding of that as she carried the beer to Ben's car.

"I shouldn't have learned at Ben's expense. You couldn't really warn me, could you, Gabby?"

"No, Lin. I'm not a shepherd, and I can't force you in any direction. At that time, all I could do was hold you."

"I felt it, Gabby," Lin said as her eyes filled with new tears, from a supply she guessed might never run dry. "You did hold me—all that time. You kept me from falling into . . . I don't even know what. But I still had to live my life, didn't I?"

"Yes. And you did. It's not possible for any of us to go through life without hurting anyone else."

"Like Ben."

"But you healed him. You made him whole again."

"Yeah, over thirty years later. Gabby, I never meant to hurt him."

"With great power comes great responsibility, Lin. Let yourself live. Accept that it takes time to learn."

"I started to learn that day. It was supposed to be nothing but fun. I was right—no one was around. The place looked deserted. The padlock on the gate looked locked, but it wasn't, and I pulled it out and swung the big gate in. With Ben's car parked down the street, we all walked in, each of us drinking a beer . . ."

* * *

"This place is awesome!" Ben said before chugging half of his beer.

"Lin, this was a great idea—we have the place to ourselves!" said Luanne after she'd taken a sip.

"I don't have a license yet," said Lin, "but I don't need one. Not here. Look at that dump truck over there. How cool would that be to drive? Anyone dare me to?"

They all dared her to drive it, and they walked over, where Lin finished her beer, handed Ben his second, and put the remaining six-pack down on the driver's side running board. She grabbed the mirror bracket and pulled herself up to peek in through the window.

"I knew it! The key's in it! Ben, hand me another beer."

He pried one out of its plastic ring and passed it up to her. She took the can, shuffled farther back along the step, and squealed the door open. She sat, wedged the can between her legs, and felt it cold and wet against her skin.

"Luanne, come on in. Everyone, climb on. I'm taking this thing for a ride!"

Lin's dad had taught her several times how to operate a manual transmission, and she'd used the clutch a couple of times in the driveway, just enough to move the car a few feet. She stretched her legs down to reach the pedals, pushed the clutch, and turned the key. The engine roared to life, and Lin popped the top of her beer and took a good drink from it.

Ben stood on the running board of the driver's side, and the two other boys rode the other side. Lin shifted, gave it some gas, and eased off of the clutch. The big truck lurched and bounced a couple of times, sputtered, and evened out into a slow crawl around the construction company's lot.

"Oh, you are such a badass!" Luanne said. "I think we should call you Ms. Mayhem after this!"

Lin rolled her window down and yelled at Ben. "Hey, I'm Ms. Mayhem!"

Luanne rolled down the passenger side window, and while the big truck stirred up a thick trail of dust, all of her friends were chanting, "Ms. Mayhem! Ms. Mayhem!"

Lin circled the yard, which now contained a cloud she'd kicked up in the still air, and returned the truck to where they'd found it. She held the clutch in as it coasted to a stop, and she switched the motor off. Her friends were cheering and laughing and giggling like small children.

Lin and Luanne both jerked their doors open, forcing the boys to the ground, and they hopped down themselves with big smiles. Lin and Ben sipped their beers and walked around behind the truck until all five stood there grinning like crazy.

It was then that Lin had her idea, one that she'd regretted for over thirty years. Ben was a good kid. He was big for his age, but mostly gentle and unassuming. She knew that he had problems at home and always made an effort to be careful to not step out of line. It was just too easy . . .

"Okay, Ben. Your turn."

She reached the key out to him. Ben shook his head.

"No, thanks. Not me, Lin."

Lin knew that Ben had a crush on her. It was obvious, and probably Luanne knew it too.

"Don't be a baby, Ben. Come on . . . just once around."

"Lin, I don't think—"

"He can do it, Luanne."

She held the key out again, and Ben started to shake his head and back away.

"Lin, he doesn't want—"

"Just take the key, Ben. You're not afraid, are you?"

"Yeah, Ben," said Floyd, "you have a license too. You can drive it."

"You guys, if he doesn't—"

"He can speak for himself, Luanne. Come on, Ben . . . just once around the yard."

"Don't be a pussy, Ben," said Lucas with a sneer.

"Yeah, don't be a pussy," said Floyd before looking to see if he'd impressed Lin or Luanne.

Lin stepped right in front of Ben and held the key up near his face. Behind her, the two boys chanted, "Pussy, pussy," and even Luanne had joined in.

Lin watched the anguish on Ben's face turn to rage. He grabbed her by the shoulders and spun her around until her back was up against a stack of banded lumber.

With her heart now racing, Lin realized she'd pushed him too far. But it was too late. She could see the desperation in his eyes. He'd become a hunted animal, one that she had pursued and cornered.

She tried to push his arms away, but he was too strong. She even tried hitting him, but he shrugged it off like it was nothing. His face was looking more angry every second. She'd pushed him too far!

"You're the pussy, Lin. I'm not driving that dumbass truck of yours, but if you're such a badass, take your shirt off. Right here, right now. Go on and do it. Show us what you got."

He began pawing at her shirt, his strong hands twisting it up, and she felt it pulling up near her waist.

"Take it off. Your jeans too. Right here."

The others took it up a notch.

"Hey," said Floyd, "I know—you're Pussy Mayhem!"

In unison, they repeated her new name, all the while fanning the flames of Ben's fury. She liked her new name, but now she saw something bad in Ben's eyes—something like she'd seen in Ray's. It started to feel that way, like having to shovel more snow, and then, Lin felt like the cornered animal, with no hope of escape.

Until a deadly tide begin to rise up inside her. She recognized it right away—it was that new big piece she'd become. It was the shark.

She knew that there was no longer any sense in resisting with her punches and shoves. Those were weak and didn't get her anywhere, but what she felt inside . . . that would surely do the job.

She quit fighting and let her arms drop to her sides. She watched as Ben's face broke into a self-satisfied smile. He reached down to the bottom hem of her t-shirt.

She didn't know why, but she felt her eyes begin to close, and the indescribable flood within her continued to rise, filling her with a sweet pressure.

She still felt Gabriel's presence, though, and understood the words that came to her: "You can choose to be kind, Lin."

The world around her had become a calm, beautiful, completely still surface. Ben and everyone else appeared frozen. Lin felt, more than she saw, unexplainable masses of something churning beneath the world, and it was flowing into her. She looked into Ben's eyes, which were now sad and scared, not angry.

The pressure reached a pleasantly unbearable level, and she felt a wave rush out from her in every direction. She saw through Ben's eyes that she stood there very still, with a bright green glow in her eyes.

There was no longer any threat. No fear. And no doubts.

She'd taken Ben's life.

Lin knew that she needed to stop his attack more than anything, so she dropped his arms to his sides. From inside his life, she sensed how truly sad and scared he'd become. She knew that she could destroy him, but she remembered that she could be kind, too, like Gabriel had told her. She could help Ben since he couldn't hurt her anyway.

She thought back to how Gabriel's warm embrace had made her feel so safe and comforted. She wrapped her arms—although she suspected she wasn't really using arms—around Ben's spirit and squeezed him just enough to take away his fear.

But it seemed to make him feel worse. She heard Ben's silent screams turn into silent shrieks.

Maybe I'm not squeezing him enough, she thought, and she wrapped her arms more tightly around him.

Things got even worse—Ben was more scared than ever!

Lin didn't know what to do, but she had an intention of stopping whatever she was doing to him, and she felt herself jerked back into her own body. From there, she saw Ben's eyes roll up high, and he collapsed to the ground.

With one hand over her open mouth and her eyes wide open, Lin took a few steps back, and Luanne followed her. She shook herself fully awake, though she knew she hadn't been asleep, and tried to listen to Luanne, but Luanne was only giggling and speaking gibberish.

She looked past Luanne to see Ben curled up in the dirt. She could see that his pants were wet, and the boys near him pinched their noses shut and laughed at him. In a few seconds, Ben struggled up to his feet, but his eyes never left the ground. He stood there shaking for several more seconds, never said a word, and began staggering to the gate.

* * *

"He left without us, Gabby. Took his car and left."

"You can't really blame him, can you, Lin?"

"No. I humiliated him. If nothing else, he smelled terrible. He was probably too embarrassed to be around anyone after that."

Gabriel waited.

"Okay, I did so much more to him, things that I only found out about just a few hours ago. I saw the damage my mayhem did to his spirit. Somehow, I wrecked him. Gabby, he lived with that ever since."

"You said he had other damage too. You weren't the only one responsible."

"Not a lot of comfort in it, though. I'm glad I could help him. I saw him smile before I left the bar."

Lin felt the engine idling a deep tone and nudged the side of the gas pedal. Racing west—that was the plan. Soon, she told herself. There was nothing to go back to anymore anyway.

"Even just what the other kids saw was bad enough, Gabby. Especially the two boys—they didn't care about Ben. They mostly just laughed about it. Not Luanne, though. She was too busy being obsessed with me. It thrilled her just to walk next to me, and it was a long walk back. It gave me plenty of time to think about it."

"Do you remember now your conclusion?"

"Yeah. Oh yeah, I sure do. That power inside scared the hell out of me. I remembered wanting only to help Ben after I'd taken control of him. I thought if I hugged him somehow, it would help. And I hurt him in some way that never should have happened. On the walk back down Lawrence and Frederica is when I made the decision."

"I remember your decision, Lin."

"It made sense, didn't it, Gabby? I mean, what else could I have done?"

"Your reasons for burying your mayhem, which of course you didn't call mayhem then, made perfect sense."

"So, that's what I did. I buried my mayhem so deep I hoped I'd never see it again. And without even trying, I lost some feelings that had been eating at me too. Feelings of guilt, Gabby. It's like I washed my power down a drain, and those feelings got dragged down with it."

"Something else too."

"Yeah, Gabby. The most important thing. I understand now why I had to forget who you really are. What you really are."

Lin made no effort to stop the hot tears streaming down her cheeks. The gas pedal had been forgotten, and she had no interest in the moon.

"You saved me, Gabby, and I forgot you for over thirty years."

She was near sobbing and could barely speak as she turned to Gabriel. Gabriel looked back with a calm love that she welcomed, but it didn't stop her tears.

"Things have happened the way they had to, Lin. We were together all that time. And you knew me. You knew me as a friend. A friend is what you needed most."

"Gabby, tell me nothing will ever make me forget you again."

Gabriel nodded and gave her a smile.

"You will never forget me again, Lin."

She wiped at her tears and found a renewed interest in the moon. It shined brightly, a full circle of white against the night sky, and she realized that thirty years in the lifetime of a world was nothing. The moon hadn't changed in all that time, and it probably never would.

She'd mastered her mayhem, and she'd gotten stronger every day, strong enough to choose to heal Ben in the bar rather than destroy him. And now, Gabriel was real again, and she remembered all of their life together. Her life was starting to make sense again. She knew that she needed it to make some kind of sense.

"By the time we'd hiked back to my house, I don't know how I did it, but I didn't remember anything about what I'd done to Ray or Ben. I knew something happened, but it was like bits of a dream or a nightmare. I couldn't explain it, and I didn't even try. How is that possible?"

"We have that ability, Lin. Traumas can be hidden for us to continue with our lives. But you should know that I helped you."

"You helped me bury my mayhem? Really?"

"Yes. It took only distracting you as often as I could to help you look away from it. We've had a lot of conversations, haven't we?"

"I can't believe you could pull that off. How could you be that patient with me? That was for over thirty years, Gabby!"

"Compared to eternity, Lin, it really is but a few grains of sand."

"It's kind of sad, though," she said and managed a weak smile.

Gabriel's eyes closed.

"It was sad to help you forget me for thirty years, Lin."

"Oh, Gabby . . ."

Lin shook her head slowly and let her tears flow again as she held the wheel and looked out into the cold night.

Chapter 7 – Falling Apart

"I got home before my parents, and I had the house to myself. A huge weight had been removed from me just knowing that Ray wasn't there. I didn't know at that time where he was, but I was sure he wouldn't be back.

"I ran up the stairs, three at the bottom, then two the rest of the way, and I closed my bedroom door behind me. It's funny that even now, I remember the number of steps. It shouldn't have been hard to ask the questions I should have been asking myself: what happened to Ray and Ben? But I never even looked in that direction."

"That's exactly what you needed then."

"That's for sure. I sat there like a kid again, a kid playing at being grown up. I put some lipstick on and fixed my hair up different ways. It was only minutes later that I felt something, I didn't know what. I wiped the lipstick off—all of it—and I let my hair drop back down. I liked it long, and I wished it were longer, but I'd lost interest in doing anything fancy with it. I tiptoed out of my room, even though I knew no one was there, and I put my mom's lipstick back.

"I remember talking to you, too, but starting then, I didn't remember who you were. I just knew my best friend was there. Everyone should have a friend like you, Gabby."

"Many do."

"Really? I'm not the only one?"

"They have friends like me for other reasons, at times when they really need comfort and encouragement. Many times, they think it's their imagination, and maybe that's okay. People shouldn't have to try to understand more than they're ready for."

"Well, I'm glad I had you in my life. I practiced flicking my hair back, because I knew there's a cool way to do it, and heard the front door open and slam shut. I heard my dad's voice and knew my parents were back home, so I took another look in the mirror, happy to not see any lipstick, and I went down to see them.

"Mom didn't look so good, but she said hi, which was more than she was doing before. Dad was happy to see me, but I remember him watching me closely. I realize now how confused he must have been. Really, what did anyone think about what happened to Ray? I remember that detective and how he looked me over. He looked at my hands real close, but he didn't find any blood. What a big mystery for all of them. For me, too, if I would have thought about it much. But after I buried my mayhem, I never again knew why that cop had any interest in me."

* * *

"Lin, how are you? Did you have fun out with your friends?"

"Yeah, Dad. We kind of cut our little adventure short, but it was nice to get out of the house."

"Why don't you have a seat," he said and patted the couch next to him. "I need to talk to you about something."

Lin froze. She stared at the couch cushion and shook her head slowly. Her arms were stiff at her sides.

"What's wrong, Lin?"

She continued to stare.

"Okay, it doesn't matter. You can stand there if you want, or you can sit somewhere else."

Lin looked away from the couch, walked over to the recliner, and sat on the edge of the seat.

"The doctor decided to start Mom on a new medication for her depression. She's not just sad—it's a real medical thing. This new medicine should help, and we're pretty hopeful she'll be better soon. I just wanted to tell you so you knew what was going on. She—"

"Roger, can you come in here a second?" her mom said from the kitchen.

Lin's dad stopped his talk, but he continued looking at Lin.

"Hang on, Baby. I'll be right back."

Lin heard their voices from the kitchen. Her mom spoke in a slow and deliberate way, and her dad sounded overly patient.

"Gabby, maybe this new thing will help my mom. I'm glad Dad takes her to the doctor."

"Yes, that can only help, Lin."

"I want my mom to be okay, Gabby."

"I know, Lin."

Lin looked up when her dad returned from the kitchen, and for the first time, she noticed the lines written across his face. His eyes were still kind, but they didn't sparkle. Not like before.

"Lin, we just need to stay patient, okay? It's a hard time for your mom, and it's going to be kind of hard for us too. We're in this together, okay, Baby?"

"Yeah, Dad. What can I do? Can I help?"

"There's not really anything you can—"

"Roger?"

"One second, Lin."

Lin's dad stood slowly and held his lower back as he headed into the kitchen.

"I'm worried about my dad too, Gabby. His back still isn't better."

"Yes, he's having a difficult time. Sometimes, all we can do is encourage people when they have problems."

"But there must be a way to help him, don't you think? My mom too?"

"You're doing more for them than you know, Lin. You're a joy to them."

The conversation in the kitchen stopped, and before her dad got back to the living room, Lin stood and moved closer to the stairs.

"I think I'm going to read for a while, Dad."

"Okay, my Lin. Thanks for being so understanding. Care to watch that show later with me? The one about deep sea diving?"

"Yeah, Dad, I don't want to miss that."

With that, she turned and took the first three steps, then the next three, then two at a time until she'd reached the top. A quick walk and a closed door gave her the refuge she needed.

"Gabby, I feel kind of bad—I wanted to get away. I don't know what to do about my mom. Or my dad. It's not fair what's happening. I want to help, but I don't know how."

"I know you want to help, Lin. Sometimes we just can't. There are no obvious things we can do."

"So, I just have to accept things?"

"I'm afraid so."

$* \quad * \quad *$

"That was kind of a sad time in my life, Gabby. I saw things falling apart. My mom wasn't getting any better, and it was dragging my dad down too. He did the best he could, but nothing he did mattered."

"Your life at school was okay, though?"

"Yeah. I think it was only because I'd buried everything about my mayhem. I don't know what I would have done with all of that on my mind."

Lin touched below her eyes lightly with her fingertips, picking up the beginning of a tear.

"With those troubling things hidden away, did you feel you lived a more normal life?"

"Yeah, I really did. Ray was gone, and I never saw him again. No one spoke of him, and I heard a couple months later that he'd killed himself. Even that didn't trigger any memories. I knew something bad happened to him, and my dad came home to find me passed out. I remembered all that evil man had done to me, but I never filled in the blanks about what ended it.

"Dad continued with his new job, but Mom had to leave hers not long after. I knew then what a bad case of depression looked like, and I think what happened with Ray kind of pushed her past some limit. But still, we got by.

"My high school days were good. I never saw Ben much—none of us did—but I had some good friends. I never would have had any if I'd remembered what was inside me. That power. So, life went on. I tried out to be a cheerleader and made the squad. I knew I liked acting, and I got pretty good at it. I managed to get lead roles in all the productions the school put on.

"Those couple of years went by quickly, and it was about time to graduate. I had some dread about that, because my dad told me we'd be moving back to Pennsylvania after school was done. I didn't want to go back. I'd gotten used to the warmer weather, and I had friends there."

"Do you remember your graduation day?"

"A little. It wasn't a big deal to me. I'd already made some college plans for back in PA, and I thought I knew what I wanted to do with my life. Life is full of surprises, though, you know? Once again, I couldn't see what else was coming."

Gabriel waited as Lin stared out through the windshield.

*　*　*

"Shortly after high school ended, that very summer, we moved back to Pennsylvania. It was because of my mom, I knew, even though no one made that clear. She was having such a rough time, and I think my dad couldn't be her only support. Back in PA, there were family members who could chip in. My dad could only do so much.

"It worked out okay for me. I took classes at Northampton and transferred later to Penn State. The semi-freedom was nice, and I could still come home for the weekends if I wanted. I was on campus in my senior year when I got the news: Mom and Dad both died in a car accident."

"I'm sorry they went so soon, Lin. I'm glad you were well on your way to a good life by then, though."

"Yeah, I was just about to graduate, and I'd still been picking up acting gigs whenever I could. It wasn't long after that that I started bounty hunting too."

"You didn't need that for the money, did you?"

"No, not really. I'd inherited their house, and I was surprised to learn that they had a pretty nice insurance policy too. So, I wasn't struggling, at least not yet."

"Then, Taylor happened?"

"Oh yeah, Taylor sure happened," Lin said with a bright smile. "Gabby, that had to be one of the happiest moments of my life: when I first looked into that baby girl's eyes. She changed my life for the better. It wasn't until much, much later that things went bad."

"Yes, I'm sorry."

"In the beginning, bounty hunting was more for the excitement of it. I liked that it was often a practical application of my acting skills. It was always fun planning out just the right approach, figuring out the best time and place, and putting it all together. I never go after the dangerous types, so it's been a pretty easy time."

"But later, it became more necessary?"

"Yeah, when Taylor got sick. She'd moved out, and I was proud of her—she was a very independent girl."

"Like her mom?"

"Yeah, I guess so, Gabby. That broke my heart when we had that big argument or whatever that was. She moved out shortly after that, and it was never the same again. And then, it didn't take long before Taylor got sick, and it was nothing anyone could figure out. They still can't.

"So, now I do the bounty hunting to help pay for the medical expenses. I could easily end up sad like Mom was all the time if I'd let myself. And if I didn't have you all that time.

"But anyway, I'm getting ahead of myself. After college, I was ready for a real job. I picked the place I wanted to work at most, sent the application, did pretty well at the interview, and got the job. I've been at Dr. Grayson's Sweet Pets ever since."

"That's very good, Lin. It's something you've cared about since you were a girl."

"It's close anyway. Ideally, I'd be some kind of marine biologist or something, but this is pretty good too."

"I can tell you enjoyed it there. Will you miss it?"

"Yeah, it's another thing I'm not happy about leaving behind, but it's not even close to being what I'll miss the most."

"Taylor?"

"Yeah, of course, I miss Taylor, but with her, it's different. We talk sometimes, but we haven't seen each other in a couple of years."

"Nomad?"

Lin shook her head a few times before answering.

"Yeah, I already miss that sweet fluffy boy."

"Jack?"

"Yeah, it's Jack. Gabby, I left Jack behind too. When I hit the gas and burned down Broadway into the sunset, I took with me the memory of how good he's been for me. It seems like that's the last I'll see of him: looking rejected and confused in my rearview mirror."

After a few moments of silence, which Lin used to stare into the night, Gabriel spoke.

"Do you remember the first time you met Jack?"

A smile appeared but not a big one. She closed her eyes and answered.

"Yeah, I sure do. I think that might have been some kind of magic too, Gabby."

Chapter 8 – Lingering Smiles

"You must be the cowboy, but I didn't see a horse hitched out front."

Lin stood next to the booth and recognized Jack Madison from his online photos. He stood right away with a smile. They both wore jeans, and Lin noticed his cowboy boots.

"That's funny. I don't really have a horse, but you probably guessed that."

Arthur's Bar & Grill had few patrons on that late Thursday afternoon. The usual crowd sat at the bar, but most tables and booths remained empty. Its location just west of Allentown looked like a good rendezvous point to both of them when they wrote to each other on the dating site.

"Yeah, I figured, but I do like the name Cowboy Jack. It's cute."

"I bet I like your name even more. How did you ever come up with that?"

"Got your attention, huh? Oh, that's a long story, Jack. Or should I think about calling you Cowboy?"

Jack got a happy smile, and his big brown eyes shined at her.

"I wish you would, and maybe I can call you Cowgirl?"

"Hmm . . . we'll see about that."

They sat in the booth with lingering smiles while they looked into each other's eyes, and when the server came around, they realized they hadn't yet thought of what to order.

"Oh, I haven't even looked yet for dinner, but I'd like a gin and tonic to start with."

"I'll have a draft," Jack said before picking up his menu. He pried his eyes away from Lin's bright green eyes and began scanning it.

She took the opportunity to get a better look at his rugged, clean-shaven face and his thick, wavy brown hair. She'd just gotten started examining his shoulders pressing against his shirt when she realized that too much silence might not be the best thing.

"What looks good to you, Jack?"

He looked up from his menu and carefully studied all of Lin's features, taking in her blond hair on each side falling down over her shoulders, her blue beret resting regally above, her red lips that were curling up into a smile from his attention, and finally her eyes. He held her gaze for a few seconds and smiled before looking down again.

"Oh, sorry. You mean the menu."

He looked back up to see Lin shaking her head slowly with a big grin.

"Yeah, Jack. Cowboy Jack."

*　*　*

"I think I kind of fell in love with him right then and there, Gabby, and I know why now: his eyes. There's never been anything but truth and honesty in his eyes. I never realized how I'd learned over the years how to see who people really are by what I see in their eyes. I think that all started with Ray and all the evil I saw in his."

"That's a very useful skill to have."

"There's nothing sneaky about Jack. I saw that right away. And that first moment, when he looked up from his menu and studied me—it was in such an innocent, honest way. He wasn't sneaking a look or leering—he was just being playful. I knew my sweater was kind of tight—I'd bought a smaller size by mistake—but I never caught him checking me out like that. He seemed to want more than anything else what he saw in my eyes."

"He's a good man, Lin. You knew that from the start."

"But I didn't know just how good. I got more clues as the dinner went on, though."

* * *

"How was your lobster? You're a big fan of seafood, I guess?"

"Yeah, especially lobster. I spent some of my childhood years in St. Simons Island, in Georgia. The few times I had fresh seafood back then, I loved it, and it's still at the top of my list."

"Do you miss living there? If nothing else, the weather must have been a lot nicer."

"Oh yeah, Jack, the weather was wonderful, and in a lot of ways, I do miss it. How about you? Have you lived in Pennsylvania all your life?"

He looked away only long enough to sip his beer, and then his eyes went right back to hers.

"Yep, all my life. All around the Allentown area too. It's not always fun working outside in the cold, though. I rebuild houses, and sometimes, I end up doing outside projects in the cold."

"You flip houses? That's pretty cool."

"Well, maybe 'flip' isn't the word. I usually don't get them done quick enough, but I like to take my time and do the best job I can."

Lin started to smile and had a provocative comment to add, but she bit her lip and kept it to herself.

"That's still pretty cool. You sound like a hardworking man, that's for sure."

"I guess. I enjoy it, though, so it's not so much like work most of the time. You work with animals?"

"Yeah, I've been with a place called Sweet Pets for quite a while now. It's good work, and I enjoy it. I like helping all the animals that we take care of. One of my big dreams was to do the same kind of work but for marine life. The ocean really made a huge impression on me when I was a kid."

"I believe that. It's a beautiful thing. Maybe you'll move closer to the ocean someday? Or at least visit it as much as you want."

"I'd like that, Jack. You probably would too."

He held her gaze for a few seconds and said, "I'm sure I would."

* * *

"Gabby, he wasn't outright flirting with me, but still, he was telling me in subtle ways how much he liked me. It was refreshing to meet a guy like that."

"You've seen enough of men that aren't so good."

"That's for sure. While Taylor was around, I never felt a real need to date. I did a little here and there, but it wasn't a serious thing in my life. Once Taylor moved out and we drifted apart, I could feel the emptiness surrounding me. And you know what? Sitting in that booth across from Cowboy Jack, I felt like maybe, just maybe, he could be the one."

"But you weren't sure?"

"No, no way. I'm not about to make a big decision that quickly."

"That was two years ago?"

"Yeah, about."

"What do you think now?"

Lin shrugged.

"I guess I'm not that quick with decisions sometimes."

"Does a heart wait for a decision, or does it know?"

"I'm not sure it matters anymore, Gabby. He looked too sad to even wave—he just stood there with the wind blowing his clothes all around. His tie too. He wore a tie for me, and I knew why."

She looked past Gabriel at the strips of concrete lit by dim moonlight. Still, not a car had passed. She had a fleeting thought that somehow time had been suspended for her to talk with Gabriel. Was that even possible? There should have been at least one car passing by.

"That first dinner with him was good, though?"

"It was wonderful, Gabby. I felt so comfortable around him. I think maybe I can be kind of difficult sometimes because I'm very independent and not too trusting. Jack was something else, though. He just seemed so accepting of me. I can't imagine him ever trying to change me in any way. Well, he never tried in the time I've known him, at least."

"It's good that you balanced the effects your mayhem had on him."

"Oh yeah, the things I put that man through! And still, his feelings for me never changed. Maybe I left him how I found him?"

"I don't think so, Lin. You've touched his heart, and there's probably no way for you to return him to who he was before you entered his life."

She turned and looked down the center of her Temt8tion's hood at the ten tiny lights. They'd only turn on if the car were accelerating a lot, except now, they each carried a faint piece of the moon. Those ten lights had burned like the fever she'd felt when she left. When she left Jack behind . . .

* * *

"I'm going to take a chance and guess that you have room for a little bit more," Jack said and laid four small chocolate bars on the table between them.

"Oh, Jack . . . I do like chocolate."

Without looking away from her eyes, he pushed three of them toward her and pulled one back for himself.

Caught off-guard, Lin could only say, "Jack, even cowboys can count better than that," and gave him a big smile.

"I can count, Lin. This is my promise to you: that you will always have three to my one."

She felt a thin film of tears in her eyes.

"And not just chocolate."

When she felt that a tear might roll down her cheek and make too big of a deal out of it, Jack showed that he'd taken that into consideration too.

"But if you're not quick enough, you'll be lucky to get even one," he said and began slowly walking his fingers toward her chocolate.

She snatched her three pieces up quickly, and a smile chased away any thought of tears.

"Oh, I'm quick enough, Cowboy Jack."

* * *

"Gabby, we've never had any bad times together. Jack is the most solid, honest, and dependable man I know. It doesn't hurt that he looks so good either."

"It's good that you managed to find each other. You've always had a lot going on in your life, Lin."

"That's for sure. There were so many things that I'd kept from him, and not because I didn't trust him. I understand things so much better now, now that I remember everything. Including you. I wasn't trying to hide things from him."

Gabriel turned to look at Lin, and she glanced over before looking back out into the night.

"Okay, some things it was by choice. Like bounty hunting. And the abuse."

"And Taylor."

"Yes, Taylor too."

"Do all those parts of your life come together as a package deal?"

"You know, that's a good way to look at it. It's all twisted together, and I never knew which parts I could pick out of the tangle and share with anyone. It felt like something big would fall apart and crash down on me."

"Was it the same with Taylor?"

"Yeah, Gabby, especially with her. I didn't even know how much I was keeping from her, but I couldn't go there. I couldn't even look at it. Now, I know why."

"Things could be better now? Now that you see it all?"

"Yeah, if I didn't just drive away from everything."

"The road number 76,"—Gabriel pointed a thumb toward the silent highway—"leads in both directions."

"Yeah, but that's back to my old life, and it's full of converts now. Almost everyone I know will be crazy about me, like John and Tommy. Gabby, I felt like I had to leave. It was a fever, a hot fever. But that was my life back there, and I left it just as fast as I could."

Lin looked to her left and saw the pine forest thick and quiet, like a barrier between her and the life she'd built for herself. She'd raced away from it, bringing her to a place where she sat in the dark with only her best friend. A friend that she could hardly believe was real.

She thought she'd better wipe at her eyes before they got any silly ideas.

"Tell me about Nomad."

A smile took over, and Lin turned to say, "Oh, that Nomad. He's unbelievable, Gabby."

"I bet you remember the day you met him."

"Oh yeah, I'll never forget. It was probably a year or so after I met Jack. This is hard to explain, but even though I felt so lucky to have Jack in my life, I felt kind of bad for him at the same time.

"I could see that he loved me already, or at least he knew he would sometime soon. He was all in, Gabby. And I . . . I had so much going on inside me. The things I remembered—like Ray—were still horrible and hard to handle, but it was more than that. My mayhem erupted just a week ago, but I think it's been brewing in there for a while. It's been pretty unsettling, and it's not something I could ever explain to Jack. Heck, I couldn't explain it to myself.

"And then, Nomad showed up . . ."

Chapter 9 – Meeting Nomad

"Lin, just relax and let me wait on you, alright?"

"You don't have to bring me coffee, Jack. You're too good to me."

"I'm happy to. I'd join you on the couch, but I'm too busy."

"It's too much, Jack. You didn't have to do that."

"Can you smell it? I cook a pretty damn good breakfast, don't you think?"

"Oh, Cowboy. Come here."

He sat next to her as she lay against pillows on the couch, and she sat up and pulled him in. She wrapped her arms around him and rubbed the solid muscles of his back. Her lips greeted his, and they lost themselves in a kiss.

"We taste like coffee, Jack."

She reached up higher and played with his wavy brown hair and looked into his eyes.

"You're sweet no matter what. I hope you're hungry. I made your omelet with the leftover lobster."

"Oh, Jack, you're wonderful."

"Guilty as charged. Breakfast will be ready in a few minutes."

She kissed him again, and he left for the kitchen. As Lin watched his arms and back muscles stretching his t-shirt, and other parts filling out his faded jeans, she took a deep breath and felt the disarray growing inside her. Something was going on, but she didn't know what.

And poor Jack—he deserved someone without secrets and with no mysterious things bubbling up.

Well, Jack will be fine, she thought and went to get dressed for work. She pulled her jeans on and hesitated when she held her baggy scrub top in front of her. It was a work day, and that's what she wore—what every coworker wore too—but she felt like tossing it to the floor. She didn't know why.

Jack likes me even in scrubs, she thought as she finished dressing and joined him at the kitchen table.

"Jack, you really did make me a lobster omelet? You're so good to me."

"Happy to make you anything you want. There are waffles too. How many? Three?"

"I can't eat that much, Jack. How about if I start with one?"

"Your wish is my command," he said and brought her a waffle, a glass of orange juice, and a fresh cup of coffee.

He took a seat, and they got started. But Lin had been watching him and feeling the uncertainty stirring inside.

"Jack, you deserve better than me."

He stopped with his mouth full of breakfast and stared at her. He shook his head while he quickly swallowed the mass of food that he couldn't take the time to chew.

"What are you talking about? You're my dream come true. You know that, right?"

"I hope so, Jack. I just feel kind of distracted lately. I don't know why. Don't tell me you haven't noticed."

"Well, you do seem a little pensive lately but not too much."

"'Pensive.' That's a good word for it. I don't even know what's distracting me. It's just a vague uneasiness. You sure you don't mind?"

She bit at her lip as she sat and looked his way.

He set his fork down and walked to her side of the table. He made her giggle when he pulled her chair away from the table and turned it. He reached one hand under her thighs and the other along the small of her back. Seemingly with no effort, he lifted her into his strong arms, and she wrapped her arms around his neck. Her giggling had stopped.

He turned a bit and leaned her toward the table. He answered her confused look by tilting his head toward her juice. She reached out and lifted the glass, took a sip, and set it back down.

"You looked like you were still thirsty."

"Oh, Jack . . ."

He carried her into her bedroom as if she weighed no more than a baby, and he laid her down gently. She backed up to give him room, and he lay down facing her. Lin waited in silence.

He reached out with both hands to touch her cheeks, then he played softly with her ears, and he ran his fingers up into her blond hair and pulled her in for a kiss.

"Jack . . . I'll be late for work . . ."

"This is all I need—just this moment with you in my arms and to give you a kiss."

She gazed into his big brown eyes and had no idea how to respond.

"Really, just doing that—I love it."

Jack's eyes got soft, and he smiled at her. She knew that he meant what he said—he always did.

"You can go to work anytime," he said and continued to look into her eyes with a contented smile.

With a laugh that resembled a growl, Lin reached to Jack's trim waist, and she found the bottom hem of his t-shirt. With his help, she peeled it up and off of him. He stood beside the bed, giving her a good look at the lean muscles built up from years of hard work, and he reached for his belt buckle.

"Of course . . . I love this too," he said with an eager smile.

Lin stared into his eyes as she began to unbutton her top. When that had been opened and pulled to each side, and Jack's eyes seemed unable to look anywhere else, she started on her jeans.

* * *

"Glad you could join us," said her boss, Dr. Grayson.

"Oh, sorry . . . running a bit late today. I hope I didn't hold anything up."

"Well, as a matter of fact, Lin, you did. It's not the end of the world, though. We just took in our new supply of orphans that need new homes."

"Oh, that was today? How many?"

"Four puppies and six kittens. They're all waiting together in Exam Room 3. They all need to be checked out and up-to-date on shots before we can find homes for them. Sound like something you'd be interested in?"

"Oh yeah, you know I would."

"Yeah, I did know. I think this might be your favorite thing about this place."

"That's for sure!"

Lin smiled and nodded and headed straight for them.

*   *   *

When she stepped into the room, it erupted in eager barking and meowing, and Lin looked from cage to cage at all the scared but hopeful faces looking back at her. Only one sat perfectly still and watched her.

She walked closer and stooped down so that their faces were level with each other, and she looked him over. He was big, almost too big for the puppy cage. His thick, red fur fluffed out in every direction, and he had the beginning of a bushy mane circling all around his neck. He sat patiently and waited.

After her quick study of him was complete, she met his staring eyes. They were big eyes, and he looked back at her without blinking. She watched as he looked calmly into her eyes and tilted his head a slight amount.

She reached a finger into the cage near his nose, and he only pressed his snout against it and held it there while continuing to hold her gaze.

Lin knew that a big, furry part of her future had begun right there in that quiet moment.

*   *   *

"We have some prospective parents coming in later, Lin. I told them all that we have four pups and six kittens, so don't start thinking you're going to run off with any of them."

"You know me too well, Doctor."

"So, you do see someone you want for your own?"

"Oh, yeah. That big puppy. There's something really special about him."

"Yeah, he'll be eating like a horse soon. I've kept it secret, but last week, I found him sitting on my porch. No crate, no note . . . just him, sitting quietly. I put out ads, and no one has claimed him, maybe because he's a Tibetan Mastiff. He's going to get big, Lin."

"How big?"

"How much food can you afford?"

"Oh my God, he's adorable. I wouldn't care how much it costs to feed him."

"Don't get your hopes up yet, okay? He's on the list sent out to possible parents, so we need to give them a chance."

"Okay, I guess I'll have to wait. But for how long? He can't stay in that little cage. He needs to run, and my backyard is fenced, and—"

"Why don't we give him a couple of days, okay? Then he's all yours . . . if you haven't changed your mind."

Lin smiled and nodded and began counting the days.

*　　*　　*

"He was going to be too big for anyone else, Lin?"

"Oh yeah, Gabby. I remember reading that his breed could grow to be huge, but even I didn't suspect Nomad would end up around two-hundred pounds!"

"And Jack was happy that you'd adopt him?"

"He seemed kind of indifferent when I told him about it. He said as long as I was happy, then it was a good thing."

"How about when Jack first met him?"

"That was a funny thing. He didn't act happy or anything else. He just seemed calm and content, like Nomad somehow fit in with his life in ways he didn't even realize. It's like he knew Nomad all his life and was just relieved to have him back again. Does that make sense? I didn't know what to make of it."

"Nomad's a very special guy. I'd say he's where he belongs."

"Oh, that's for sure, Gabby. He seemed to already know his way around my house, and we just fell into a good routine right away. He's too good to be true."

"Oh, I think he's every bit as good as he seems. I'm glad he found you. And Jack."

"He found us?"

"The important thing is that you're together. It sounds like he's the perfect one for you. And Jack too."

"I'm still sad and embarrassed that I tried my mayhem on him yesterday. I don't know what I was thinking about."

"I believe Nomad understands more than you think. He's forgiven you, hasn't he?"

"He did, but I left him too."

"Yes. You did what you felt you had to do, Lin. Our true paths become obvious to us when we need to make those choices, if we'll only take the time to look. You chose what you needed to in that moment."

"Doesn't make it any easier."

"Yes, I know."

"So, Nomad fit right in with me and Jack, and it was only a couple of months ago that I decided to change my wardrobe."

"Did Jack like your new style?"

"Yeah, Gabby. He sure did."

Lin stared out into the still night hugging the highway and weaving itself all through the forest to her left. The moon had traveled some more, and it shined brightly, but it seemed to respect the night and gave it unchallenged authority beneath the pines.

And she still liked imagining that it had always watched her. A silent and timeless companion that followed its own path and schedule, showing itself in her life at times of its own choosing. Like that one hot August night last summer when Jack came to pick her up for a night out. The lucky boy had no idea what he'd find . . .

Chapter 10 – Dressing Up

Lin peeked out from behind her living room curtains and watched Jack steer his pickup into her driveway. When he climbed down and slammed his door, she saw his fit good looks dressed up in simple jeans and a dress shirt, and his cowboy boots gave her a smile.

She looked down at her new footwear and realized that she had no idea what to expect. She turned to glance at Nomad lounging across the couch and shrugged, but he only yawned and laid his big head back down.

When Jack passed the window without seeing her, it warmed her heart to see the bouquet he carried as he walked up on her porch to rap on the door.

Such a gentleman, she thought. What on Earth will he think of me? Oh well, too late now . . .

Lin turned the knob and pulled the door in, letting it swing out of the way on its own to give Jack a good view. His eyes grew almost as big as Nomad's as he looked her up and down and side to side, and finally, he found her eyes and smiled like a kid about to ride his first roller coaster. She decided right then to make sure that he wouldn't be disappointed.

He still hadn't said a word, but he looked down enough to see Lin's white long-sleeved blouse, top buttons open and, she believed, making him wish she'd pop a few more. The bottom hem of the shirt fell just over the top band of her tight black skirt. It clung to her like not much more than hot plastic wrap, and he didn't have to look very much farther to find the skirt's bottom hem. And just beneath the hem of her short skirt, her bare thighs stretched down strong and smooth and almost dared him to look away. Somehow, he found the will, and he followed her long legs down to see her new favorite black heels. They were high and spiky, and thin straps circled around her ankles.

He did a slow, careful scan back up over every detail, his eyes smiling at every part of her, and he again found her eyes.

"Hi, Jack. How the heck are you?"

She never knew him to stutter, but he appeared to be on the brink of starting that day.

"Lin, what . . . I mean . . ."

"You like, Jack?"

"You . . . you're so—"

"This is my new style, Jack. You can either tell me I'm crazy, or you can come here and kiss me."

With his options narrowed down to two simple choices, he made a quick decision. He closed the distance and reached around her waist, still holding the flowers in one hand. Lin's heart fluttered at Jack's tentative touch. He held her gently around her waist, and his smile didn't fade as he gave her a kiss to show her that he'd never tell her she was crazy. Up on her heels, with her arms over his shoulders, she only needed to turn her head up slightly to offer him her lips, and when he pulled her up against him, she knew for sure that she had his complete approval.

"I'm dressed up, but that doesn't make me fragile, Jack."

She felt his strong arms tighten around her and smelled the bouquet as he squeezed her close for another kiss. Then, he moved his hands down to her waist and held her out from him. She watched as he looked down to the open buttons of her blouse, and she felt his free hand let her go. He reached up and opened another button before looking into her eyes, and she let out a deep sigh.

"Don't stop, Jack . . ."

He opened two more buttons, smiled at her choice to wear only the blouse, and looked back into her eyes.

"Lin, you are absolutely gorgeous," he said with a gigantic smile. "I like your new style."

She reached down to his waist and pulled him close so that their hips pressed into each other and said, "I can tell, Jack."

After reaching over and slamming the door behind him, she found the deadbolt and turned it with a decisive clunk.

"No dinner tonight?" he said with a grin.

"Oh, Jack . . . are you hungry? I think I might have just what a hungry boy like you needs."

With a low growl, he swept her up in his arms and held her there, waiting for a kiss. She played with his wavy brown hair for only a second before he lifted her closer and kissed her deeply. She felt locked into his arms and knew that he could hold her all day if needed.

He finally broke the kiss, and Lin said, "You know, Jack, you haven't seen every little thing I have on."

He shook his head with a grin and began a solid walk through her foyer and down the hall. Lin needed to keep her heels from hooking on several corners, and they entered her bedroom. He laid her softly on the thick blanket and took a moment to look down on her like a kid in a candy store.

"Stay, Jack."

He seemed to have forgotten how to smile as he stared down on her lying on her back, slowly opening the few buttons still holding her blouse together. When she'd finished the last one, she held each side and slowly pulled them apart as she arched her back, all the while staring into his eyes. She continued working at the thin material until she'd pulled it down over each shoulder and slipped her arms free.

"Almost there, Jack."

Jack stared, speechless.

She reached down for the top band of her skirt and began working it over her hips. When she'd tugged it down to her thighs, she paused and said, "Oops . . . I guess you did see everything I'm wearing."

Jack shook his head with a big smile, but he waited as patiently as he could.

She pulled her knees forward and slid the skirt up and over them and pushed it to her ankles, where her new shoes kept it from falling off completely. From there, she extended her legs straight up until her heels were high above the bed.

"Oh, Jack, would you be a sweetheart and help take this off of me?"

"Oh, God yeah."

He reached over from beside the bed, pulled her skirt up and over her black heels, and tossed it across the room. She stretched her legs out on the blanket and reached for the bouquet still in his hand.

His trembling hand shook the flowers as he handed them to her.

"Thanks for the flowers, Jack. That was very sweet of you."

Jack shook his head and struggled to speak. Both of his fists clenched and opened. His eyes seemed unable to decide which part of Lin they wanted most. Somehow, he settled on her eyes.

"Well, you're very sweet yourself."

Lin took a breath of the bouquet, then rested both of her hands on the pillows above her head.

"Do you like sweet things, Cowboy?"

* * *

The sun had spent itself and retired, and between the two of them, the only clothing that remained was Lin's black heels. Everything else, including the flowers, lay scattered across the bed and the wood floor of Lin's bedroom. They awoke in a tight embrace, in a room lit only by a full moon peeking in through an open window that let in a few cool breezes.

She ran her hands over his hard muscles and felt his breaths calm, but his skin still hot from the passion they'd chosen over dinner. She saw his closed eyes and a faint smile despite his fatigue, and she glanced past him to see the moon revealing itself as a few wispy clouds fled to the north. She took the time to look at how the pale rays highlighted the lean muscles of the exhausted man lying on his side next to her.

With her right hand resting on his cheek, she said, "Oh my, Jack. You really meant it."

"What's that?"

"Three pieces of chocolate, like you said when we first met. I just love getting three, Jack."

His eyes didn't open, but he smiled and said, "Good, because I love you getting them."

She kissed him, smiled, and said, "I like that we see eye to eye on numbers, Jack."

His chest muscles expanded out with his relaxed breaths, and Lin reached out to run her fingers over every defined feature. His eyes still didn't open, but his smile grew.

She shimmied down, slid her left hand under his waist, held his hip with her right, and rested her head against his chest. She felt it warm and solid, Jack's breaths steady and deliberate, and she pulled him in close until her skin rubbed against every part of him.

He reached over and found her hair, and her heart melted as he caressed her gently, twirling it around before laying it back over the sheets. He reached up higher and found her ear, which he squeezed and played with before he worked his fingers into her hair. He pulled her tight against his chest, and she felt it hard against her. She looked up to see his big brown eyes looking intently into hers.

"We don't always have to be eye to eye though, do we, Cowboy?"

Chapter 11 – Driving Fast

"I'm glad I changed my wardrobe, and I've never regretted it, but I have to wonder—were you with me every minute of every day?"

Lin looked away from the moon and her sweet memories and turned toward Gabriel.

"No, I was with you only when you needed me, Lin. There were many times when I had no knowledge of your life. If I sensed you were in danger, or about to make a difficult choice, or even if you wanted to talk, I would join you."

"That's good to know because I still had to live my life. I guess you knew that, huh?"

"Yes, Lin, of course. Did Jack like the change?"

"Oh my God, yeah, he sure did."

"And that all started with that one little comment I made about your clothing?"

"I think that's what pushed me, Gabby, but no, I think it was time. Your comment kind of helped to shatter a wall built up inside me. When I shopped for the new clothes, I remember that I started out with much more modest goals. I found some heels that weren't nearly so high, and they looked good, but they didn't seem quite right for me. I went on from there, and—"

Lin stopped herself and paused.

"Oh, you know what, Gabby? I just realized this. While I was shopping, I started feeling like that kid that stole her mother's lipstick, way back before I used my mayhem to destroy Ray. So, I grabbed some taller heels and found I could barely stand in them, but I knew I'd learn. That's what it felt like—I was that young girl again, playing dress up."

"And Jack likes it?"

"No doubt about it. He's so sweet, though. I know he likes me just fine in ordinary clothes. I think when I dress up like that, he picks up on how I feel about it, and that's a big part of what makes him happy. Of course, he likes me looking sexy too—there's no denying that."

"There's a famous song about how a river might change its course, but it always reaches the sea."

Lin looked back out into the darkness.

"I think that's me, Gabby. Finding and then burying my mayhem changed my course, but now . . . this feels right. Like I'm still finding who I am—I'm finding my sea. And since when do you know anything about songs?"

"I don't know of many—only the good ones. The ones that sprang from the heart."

"How can you tell?"

"Artists often follow paths of quiet anguish. The miracle of life is like a flame to them, and they devote their lives to holding that burning mystery. From the heat of it, they sometimes cry out, and to us it is great music. Or writing. Or dance. If what they have created touches your heart, they've given you a piece of that mystery, that miracle that they struggle to know."

Lin saw that Gabriel was now staring out into the night, and she hesitated before speaking.

"Gabby, have you helped others besides me?"

"Yes, a few. But not lately. And not for the same reason. You're quite rare."

Gabriel turned, and they shared a smile, and Lin wondered if she'd ever understand her impossible friend.

"How about this fast car of yours?"

Lin looked at the dashboard and instruments and felt the plush leather seat cradling her curves just right.

"You know, I'm sure it had a lot to do with my new style . . ."

*   *   *

Lin parked, swung the door open, and stepped into the early September sun warming the bank's asphalt parking lot. She slammed the door and tried to pull her short black skirt down, but there didn't seem to be enough material.

Oh well, she thought, as she flicked her long blond hair back over her thin pink blouse and aimed for the entrance, with her heels clicking smartly.

She found no lines inside, and the two young male tellers seemed to be competing for her business. Each called out to her, but one of them, the better looking one she thought, didn't hide his approval as he glanced down quickly, then back up to her eyes. Lin removed her sunglasses and held them up near her shoulder as she walked over to him.

"What can I do for you?"

"I'd like to make a deposit, but I haven't filled out the ticket yet. Do you think you could—"

"Yes, of course, I have one right here. Look, and here's a pen too."

She took the deposit slip and pen from him, filled it out and signed it, then passed him a thick stack of bills.

"And could you print the balance out too, please?"

"Oh sure, yeah, of course, happy to . . ."

Lin took her receipt and turned to leave. She wasn't sure why she wore such a smile, but she figured swaying her hips a little bit more than usual might be a good idea.

Back in the sun, she stopped and crossed her arms as she stood staring at her modest old car. She replayed a memory of her and Jack that first night that she'd dressed up in her new style, when she'd nearly driven him crazy, and she knew that her new clothes were a big part of the fun. She even had a fleeting thought of the young man in the bank. She was just sure that he'd watched her every step as she'd walked away from him.

She knew right then that that old car didn't fit her new style.

Nope, she thought, that car just won't do.

* * *

After she'd rolled down the driver's side window, Lin started the engine and headed for Philadelphia. She wasn't in the mood for a domestic variety, or even an average high-end import. She knew just what she wanted, and it had to be sleek and stylish and very fast.

She pulled in and shut the motor down, ignoring the weird feelings inside. She'd told Jack that she'd felt distracted, but she knew that wasn't right. Something was going on. Things were changing. She pushed it aside to focus on why she'd come to this particular showroom.

Outside of her car, she straightened her skirt as well as she could and walked over to the shiny black Temt8tion, the one she'd read about in the paper. This dealership had the only one east of the Mississippi, and it was loaded. She knew the price, and the thought of having to step up the bounty hunting didn't appeal to her. But the prospect of going that fast, and looking that good while doing it—that was irresistible.

"Your style is perfect for that car," said the salesman walking toward her. He wore a casual sport coat, without a tie, and appeared to be in his early thirties. Lin observed him only long enough to see that he managed to look her in the eye before she turned to the car.

"I'm Jerry, and I have the best car for sale anywhere. This baby right here."

"I won't argue with that, Jerry. I'm Lin. I read about this car. Just how fast is it?"

"How fast do you want to go?"

Lin got a big smile and said, "Sometimes, real fast. I read about these lights."

She pointed at the ten tiny lights evenly spaced and molded smoothly into the centerline of the hood.

"It's a unique feature to the Temt8tion. They're for when you're accelerating really quick, so really, there's no reason to put them on any other car."

"That's for sure!"

They shared some laughter, and Lin said, "What's this paint color called?"

"Oblivion Black."

Lin gazed into the hood bathed in bright sunlight, and she found herself lost in the flawless reflection.

"Oblivion. Yep, that's for sure. And the interior?"

"All black leather, and the seats have so many adjustments, you can make them fit you perfectly."

He didn't hide his glance down at Lin's short skirt, her trim waist, and cleavage above the open buttons of her blouse, and Lin fought to contain her smile.

Hmm, she thought, a little innocent attention isn't so bad. It does chase away that nagging feeling inside.

He'd recovered and was again looking into her eyes, and she took a walk around to the passenger side. He followed close behind, and she was aware of her hips swaying in her tight skirt. She might even have exaggerated her motions a bit—she couldn't be sure.

Rounding the rear fender, she noticed that the passenger window was down, and a fun idea popped up out of nowhere.

Why not? she thought. No real harm, right?

She stood a couple of feet from the car and put her forearms on the window frame with her hands inside, and she kept her legs straight as she leaned in to take a look inside. She felt her skirt riding up a little and grinned at the smell of the leather and the sudden silence of the sales guy.

She waited there, taking her time to study the interior. Still, the man remained hushed, and Lin could only imagine what was on his mind.

While inhaling the smell of her new car, the one that she already knew she'd soon purchase, she shifted her weight from one leg to the other several times, and she realized that dressing sexy was good, and doing just a little bit of teasing was even better.

A girl's got to have some fun, she told herself.

"It looks absolutely perfect," she said over her shoulder.

"Yeah, it sure does."

Lin worked herself back out of the car and faced the salesman as she gave her skirt a tug.

"I'd sure like to take it for a ride."

"So would I. I mean, it's a dream to drive—you won't be disappointed. The key's in it."

"Don't you want to hold my license or anything?"

"You don't look like a car thief to me," he said with a grin.

What exactly do I look like? she thought and quickly thanked herself for not asking it out loud.

"Wonderful, and I'll definitely hit the highway for a couple of exits."

"Have fun. The cops will never catch you."

*　*　*

She'd just finished the second strap around her ankles and heard Jack tapping on her front door. Her heels clicked on the polished wood floors as she swung her bare legs through the house's cool air.

"Jack, we should get you used to walking in, don't you think?"

"Alright, but really, I just relived that first day I came to pick you up, when you were . . . when you'd first dressed—"

"Like this? You still like it, Jack?"

His growl and squeeze and kiss were his reply, and Lin let his strong arms move her and hold her however he wanted. When it seemed that he'd decided to let her catch her breath, she pressed him into the wall with her hips and gave him a quick kiss. Still captive within his arms, she spun around and bent over just enough to push him again into the wall. She grabbed his hands, pulled them around her waist, and found soft places for each of them.

"Oh, Lin. My God."

She felt him trying to find her neck to kiss, so she pulled her hair to one side and let it drop across his right hand.

"I have something to show you, Cowboy. I think you'll like it. Interested?"

She didn't need to ask. She sensed his enthusiasm as she leaned into him again.

"Anything. Anything at all, my Cowgirl."

"Good, but I think I'd like this attention a while longer."

He squeezed her and kissed the back of her neck as she rubbed into him.

"If you don't mind. This feels good, Jack. You make me feel good . . ."

She heard a contented sigh, and he found an ear, which he nibbled and kissed. She felt some vague uncertainty somewhere inside, but she ignored it. Being close to Jack always helped.

She felt around behind her with her left hand and found Jack's belt. She brushed each of his arms off of her and took a few steps, towing him behind her.

"You don't mind coming with me, do you, Jack?"

She began leading him toward the kitchen.

He laughed. "Never. In the kitchen?"

"Mm . . . maybe next time, Jack."

She pulled him through the kitchen and down the short hall to the garage. Her heels tapped against the wood and echoed through the quiet house, with only the sound of Nomad barking in the backyard. She turned and leaned her back into the door to the garage and pulled him in for another long, deep kiss. Then, she pushed him back and saw his eyes staring into hers as he shook his head with a big grin.

"You have no idea what to expect, do you, Jack?"

"Not a clue."

She stepped to one side, flipped the light switch, and turned the knob. She pulled the door in, and Jack gazed into the garage with his mouth hanging open.

"That's yours? You bought that?"

"Yeah, Jack. It's all mine. Like it?"

"Oh, hell yeah!"

He jumped down the two steps and stood looking at Lin's new Temt8tion sparkling under the ceiling lights. For a few seconds, he just grinned and shook his head.

"That's really your new car, Lin?"

"Seems about right for a woman like me, wouldn't you say?"

He looked up at her still two steps above him and reached for her hips. He looked into her eyes and said, "Your car should at least try to be as hot as you."

His hands slid down to her thighs, and he said, "Hey, why don't you pose with it? That's a classic shot. Come on."

He held her hand as she stepped to the garage floor, and he led her to the front of the car. They both took in the deep black shine and the heavy silver Temt8tion logo at the point of the hood. He nudged her to stand next to the emblem, and he stepped back to take in the view.

"Damn. That's definitely your car, Lin. What a perfect pair."

"Oh, Jack, you mean this pair?" she said and started to unbutton her blouse.

He took a step closer, and she said, "No, Jack. I'm posing for you, remember? Just stand back and enjoy it."

"Alright, I will definitely enjoy it."

She continued popping the buttons, and when the last one had opened, she pulled both sides down and made sure he remembered there was nothing beneath it. He stared to the left, then the right, then back to the left, then up to her eyes.

"Mm . . . I think the cold air in here might be getting to me, Jack. I hope you don't mind?"

Jack didn't mind, and his smile told her so.

She held the shirt near its collar and slid it back over her shoulders, and it held halfway down her arms for a few seconds, then she let it drop onto the car's hood. He began to take a step forward, and she pointed at him. He stopped.

"I knew it, Jack. The cold—never fails. That's not such a bad thing, though, is it?"

Jack only shook his head slowly while staring.

She sat on the cool metal of the hood and leaned back on it, resting with her arms propping her up. She planted her heels firmly on the concrete.

"Come here, Jack."

She moved her legs apart enough to give him room to stand. When he stood before her, she sat up and helped him out of his shirt. She was so close that her breath landed hot on his chest. She looked up into his eyes and unhooked his buckle, slid the belt out of the loops, and tossed it across the garage.

"Oh, Jack, it sure doesn't take much for this skirt of mine to ride up."

He took a quick look down.

"No, it sure doesn't. It's already up pretty high."

She popped open the big brass button on his jeans and looked up into his eyes.

He gently touched her hair on each side, and though he smiled, his eyes stared intently.

"And you know . . . I don't remember if I put anything on under it."

His fists closed tight around her hair.

"Oh, now I remember. It's only the skirt, Jack."

She saw that he shivered, and she guessed that it wasn't from the cool air of the garage.

She leaned back, and her hair ran through his hands as he stood there shaking his head and grinning. She laid herself flat on the hood and reached up with both hands to hold onto the edge near the windshield.

Still looking into his eyes, she said, "You like the car, Jack?"

"God, Lin. Yeah."

"Take me for a ride, Cowboy."

Chapter 12 – Holding On

"I bought that car only a couple of months before I left for the assignment in Erie. I'll never forget when I first showed it to Jack. I think it was all kind of overpowering for him."

"In a good way, though?"

"Oh, yeah. And the day after I got back from the trip to St. Simons, I drove off. I even got every hood light to turn on. You really have to accelerate for that, Gabby."

"You've had quite a week, Lin."

"Oh, I can't even believe everything that's happened. But I made it through all that. I survived it all."

"And you just revisited some important times in your life. I'm glad you shared that with me."

"I've been sharing my life with you for over thirty years! But I know what you mean. This is different. We're in my car, and we're sitting and talking with each other. We've only sat and talked that one time before, and that was right after I destroyed Ray."

"Yes."

"We got as far as you telling me your name, and I felt so safe and loved that it overwhelmed me. It's still overwhelming, Gabby."

Lin poked at the beginning of a tear and looked out through the windshield. The silence and stillness of the world outside her Temt8tion seemed to her to be some natural result of Gabriel becoming real again. As if the whole world had stopped to celebrate it, knowing all that Gabriel had done for her.

She fought to keep a sob from bubbling up.

"And now, you're holding on, Lin?"

"What do you mean?"

"To that string."

"What string? What are you talking about?"

"You might always be like a balloon adrift, Lin. Life is like that if we don't hang on to things in a panic. Living with faith takes strength, but it allows us to follow our true path."

She turned to face Gabriel and shook her head slowly. A smile appeared, and her green eyes shined.

"Yes, Gabby. I've looked back on enough of that string to get a good hold on it. I'll never let it go again, and I'll carry those memories to anchor me wherever I go. Thanks. You're still taking care of me."

"I knew you'd find a place of peace after all you've been through. And that's very good, but . . ."

Gabriel paused.

"But what, Gabby?"

Gabriel turned to look at her.

"Like I told you before, we've only begun."

Lin's smile evaporated, and she shook her head and stared at her unexplainable best friend.

ENJOY THE STORY?

Thank you for reading! Please consider leaving a review and/or a rating at your favorite bookseller or with your favorite book club. Help your fellow readers meet Lin Finity!

For more about Edward Allen Karr and his books, visit:

www.lakesideletters.com

And follow him at:

Facebook: EdwardAllenKarr

Instagram: Edward_Allen_Karr

ABOUT THE AUTHOR

Edward Allen Karr was born, raised, and continues to reside in Ohio, USA. His adult life has followed a meandering path, ranging from working an automotive assembly line to designing space flight hardware. And through all of it, he's seen that life is a captivating and ultimately unexplainable endeavor. His writing seeks to add a splash of wonder to a world already awash in it.

Lin Finity returns for more magic, adventure, and romance in:

Lin Finity And The Words Unspoken
Fringes Of Infinity Book Two

www.lakesideletters.com

Next in time in the Fringes Of Infinity world:

Lin Finity And The Words Unspoken (Book Two)

A DEADLY SCROLL bearing the Words of God.
An EVIL MANIAC seeking one who can read it.
LIN FINITY — Beautiful, powerful . . . and hunted.

Running from the trail of her mayhem, Lin has left her old life behind. But not for long. She's ready to face her future, and there's much more magic to learn. With Gabriel's help.

The Shield has been waiting for centuries for anyone with enough power to read the Scroll. If Lin won't come willingly, the diabolical group will try to force her. Everyone is in danger: her boyfriend Jack, her new friend Lee . . . even her dog, Nomad. Lin must survive their onslaught and read the Scroll . . . and not let it destroy her.

Along the way, her romance with Jack heats up, she discovers the truth of her daughter's illness, and she learns the Words of God. As they were understood by the Scroll's creator long ago.

WORDS that came UNSPOKEN.
WORDS Lin should have left UNSPOKEN.